The Museum of Future Mistakes

Winner of the
BOA Short Fiction Prize

The Museum of Future Mistakes

STORIES

James R. Gapinski

AMERICAN READER SERIES. NO. 44
BOA EDITIONS, LTD. * ROCHESTER, NY * 2025

Copyright © 2025 by James R. Gapinski

All rights reserved
Manufactured in the United States of America

First Edition
23 24 25 26 7 6 5 4 3 2 1

For information about permission to reuse any material from this book, please contact The Permissions Company at www.permissionscompany.com or e-mail permdude@gmail.com.

Publications by BOA Editions, Ltd.—a nonprofit corporation under section 501 (c) (3) of the United States Internal Revenue Code—are made possible with funds from a variety of sources, including public funds from the Literature Program of the National Endowment for the Arts; the New York State Council on the Arts, a state agency; and the County of Monroe, NY. Private funding sources include the Max and Marian Farash Charitable Foundation; the Mary S. Mulligan Charitable Trust; the Rochester Area Community Foundation; the Ames-Amzalak Memorial Trust in memory of Henry Ames, Semon Amzalak, and Dan Amzalak; the LGBT Fund of Greater Rochester; and contributions from many individuals nationwide. See Colophon on page 162 for special individual acknowledgments. Any use of this publication to "train" generative artificial intelligence (AI) technologies to generate text is expressly prohibited.

Cover Art: "The Love Affair" by Kellette Elliott
Cover Design: Sandy Knight
Interior Design and Composition: Isabella Madeira
BOA Logo: Mirko

BOA Editions books are available electronically through BookShare, an online distributor offering Large-Print, Braille, Multimedia Audio Book, and Dyslexic formats, as well as through e-readers that feature text to speech capabilities.

Cataloging-in-Publication Data is available from the Library of Congress.

BOA Editions, Ltd.
250 North Goodman Street, Suite 306
Rochester, NY 14526
www.boaeditions.org
A. Poulin, Jr., Founder (1938-1996)

For Uma and all the best, most impulsive, vibrant mistakes we'll make in the future.

Contents

The Museum of Future Mistakes	9
When the Astronauts Landed in Our Neighborhood	21
Sharon's Lover is Dissipating	25
Saw Act	29
Kitten Egg	37
Hospital Story	39
Delilah	43
My Fingernails Are Haunted	51
The Gull Bone Index	57
Evolution of Apartments	59
Brother and Not-Brother	61
Migratory Patterns	69
Fruit Rot	79
The Last Dinosaurs of Portland	99
Kitchenly Perfection	113
Three-Month Autopsy	117
The Elevator Elf	127
Physical Therapy	143
Karol's Cleaners Will Clean Anything	153
Tuxedos and Evening Gowns	155
Acknowledgments	157
About the Author	159
Colophon	162

The Museum of Future Mistakes

I have a gold membership for the Museum of Future Mistakes. If you have a local zip code, membership is twenty percent off. The museum is huge, filled with everybody's mistakes—line art of broken condoms, still life of bad takeout, a retrospective on poorly planned camping trips. I usually breeze through these displays until I find my own rotating exhibit, nestled in an alcove with good lighting.

My exhibit has helped me avoid so many mistakes. A marble bust of me puking outside the karaoke bar helped me pace myself last Saturday. Before that, there was a painting of a one-star Amazon review—I removed that cardigan from my cart pronto. Abstract paintings can be initially frustrating—but they're also intriguing because it's like a game to figure out what mistake I'll make. In those cases, the placard with a description and info about the artist helps. I love the glimpses that the Museum of Future Mistakes provides. It helps me live my best life without having to fuck around with motivational Instagrammers.

Today, I'm less excited about what I see: a statue of my girlfriend Devin. The statue is vaguely Grecian, with thick muscles and stout haunches, exposed breasts, a fig leaf covering her crotch. Her fingers are stretched skyward as if to say *Follow me into oblivion!* Despite the otherwise regal appearance, she's wearing tennis shoes, and her favorite pair of plaid socks are carved into her ankles.

I look at the informational card next to the statue. It was sculpted by *Anonymous* and donated by *Anonymous*. The title is simply *Devin*, and the description reads *A depiction of your girlfriend, a colossal mistake*. The museum curator isn't prone to hyperbole. I've never seen the word *colossal* attached to any other mistake here. Most descriptions talk about the event or object, and they end by simply stating *This is a mistake*. I reread the one-sentence note again, looking for a clue that's not there. I need to know why Devin and I fall apart. With the other mistakes, I've been able to make course corrections. How can I do that here? The only option seems to be dumping Devin before our relationship collapses.

"Excuse me," I call to the nearest security guard.

"Yes, may I help you?" he says in a kind tone. His bald head glistens in my alcove's good lighting.

"Where did this come from?" I ask.

The guard leans forward, his hands folded neatly behind his back. He peers at the small sentence for a while before announcing, "It's an anonymous gift to the museum by an anonymous sculptor. It seems that dating Devin is a colossal mistake."

"I know that. I mean—" I start to say, but I'm not sure what I mean. I don't expect this guard to have any additional answers. "Can I talk to the curator?"

"She's out today. She's scouting new talent," the guard tells me.

"Can I see her when she's back?"

"Do you have business to discuss? Are you an art dealer?" he asks.

"I'm a gold member," I say.

The guard smiles as if he thinks that's a joke. Then his face hardens. "Anybody can be a gold member. It costs twenty bucks—sixteen if you're local. The curator is a busy woman."

"Okay, thanks," I say, but I'm not sure why I'm thanking him. The guard walks back to his corner, his bald head muted again as he waits for more upset people to accost him about their mistakes. I consider the statue a while longer. It has impressive detail. The fingers alone must've taken hours—splayed wide, with a finely chiseled outline along the nails. This project must've been commissioned. Somebody really wanted this mistake documented.

I go through our eleven-month relationship in my head: we met at the wine and cheese mixer; we exchanged numbers and got coffee together; we chatted for hours and found we had similar tastes in movies, books, and music; we got dinner and talked about our family drama; we fooled around at her place; we went to concerts; we met friend-groups and everybody got along; we tried some new stuff in bed, and we both liked it; we went on hikes; we had picnics; we saw more movies based on aforementioned similar tastes; we talked about career goals; we moved in together. This most recent development seems the most potentially toxic. We've only lived together a month. I wonder if that is the mistake—but then why didn't the artist make a diorama of our new apartment? Also, the museum shows future mistakes, not past ones. No, this statue implies that the problem is Devin, not the circumstances.

My phone vibrates. A text from Devin reads *Lunch?*

It's my day off, but she's at work. She must know I'm downtown and close enough to meet. Is she one of those creepy, controlling people who tracks their partner's phone? The moment of speculation lingers. I glance around to see if I'm being followed. Some batshit crazy girlfriends will hire private investigators. I saw a TV show about it once.

Where at? I text back.

Somewhere sit-down. Maybe that new Indian place? she replies.

Normally, we hit up the food trucks. She must have bad news. A sit-down restaurant seems more appropriate. Is she dying? No, that can't be it. That would be tragic but not a mistake. Am I dying? No, she couldn't know that before me. Unless she poisoned me. But that's absurd. It's just a statue. I walk to the Indian restaurant, and I repeat to myself: "It's just a statue. It's just a statue. It's just a statue."

"Huh?" Devin says. She's already seated, munching on a papadum.

"Nothing. Never mind."

"Statue? So you went to the museum?" she asks, but she must already know the answer.

"Yes," I say.

"So what did you learn? Should we cancel our movie night?"

"Why? What's wrong?" I ask, blood pulsing through my temples, anticipating an epic breakup speech on the verge of Devin's tongue. I try to calm myself. This is for the best. The Museum of Future Mistakes knows we're doomed—better to end it rather than drag this out.

"Calm down," she says, raising her hands in protest. Her splayed fingers remind me of the statue. "Nothing's wrong. I just thought the museum might've told you the movie sucks. I've been reading some Rotten Tomatoes reviews. We might want to pick a different one."

"Oh, okay," I say, and my stress level dips.

"So what was the statue? You seem on edge. Big mistake this time?"

"Colossal," I say, and I regret saying it because she'll want to know more.

Devin raises her eyebrows and leans forward in anticipation, but she doesn't say anything. We sit in silence for a while. I grab a papadum and take a bite. I avoid eye contact, and she finally leans back. "Alright, you don't have to tell me. Just avoid whatever it is. Don't want a *colossal* mistake on your hands." She laughs and opens her menu. "Palak paneer sounds good. You?"

  I look at my menu and pretend to read it. I know this can't continue. I either need to break up with Devin, or I need to get more answers about the statue. The uncertainty of this mistake prevents me from doing anything but panicking as Devin tells me about the latest drama with Margot, her Human Resources friend at work. Devin frowns and asks, "Are you listening?" I feel like each lapse in my attention is another limping step toward our relationship's inevitable doom.

I find the curator's name, Rhea Cieślak, on the Museum of Future Mistakes website. I find her face on LinkedIn. I find her current location when she tweets a picture of her extra-large mocha—it's a local coffee shop frequented by artsy hipsters, which makes sense. The caption reads *Can't meet a client without my afternoon pickup! #caffeine #mocha #coffeeslut*.

  I get on the next bus. The café is close—two stops away. I think about what I'll say to her. I can't ask for information about anonymous artists and donors right away. That will never work. I have two options. *Option One*: appeal to her sense of empathy and tell her how this is poised to wreck my relationship. *Option Two*: pretend to be an art critic or buyer who has taken a special interest in the statue. The bus grinds to a halt near the café, and I'm still not sure which course to pursue.

  Rhea's sitting at a table near the back, a spot-on replica of her LinkedIn profile, tight curls and all—and she might even be wearing the same blouse. I mumble some possible opening salvos to myself. She's eating a huge handmade marshmallow alongside her artisanal mocha. She's tearing off goopy bits and licking the excess from her sticky fingers. I slide into the chair across from her. She looks up and fidgets with her glasses, a trail of marshmallow residue clinging to the frames. "You must be the artist," she says with a smile.

"Yes," I lie, glad that a third option has insisted upon itself.

"Would you like anything?" Rhea asks. "On me, of course."

"No, thanks," I say.

"I love the work samples you sent," she says before gulping from her huge mocha mug.

"Thanks, I love your collections. The museum is so—" I'm not sure what to say about the museum. I realize that I've rarely appreciated it from an artistic perspective before. I'm more interested in the subject matter than the craft.

"Visceral?" Rhea offers.

"Yes, visceral. It's raw. Unfiltered," I say, and Rhea smiles. "Like the best kombucha. Totally unfiltered," I add, and I regret this comparison. Her smile droops. She takes another deep gulp.

"Did you bring any new work?" she asks.

"Yes," I say, and I reach into my pocket to see what's available. I give her a crumpled receipt.

She places it gently on the table between us. "Fascinating," she says, leaning in close for a better look. "But whose mistake is it?"

"Devin Shaw," I say.

"Ah, yes, her exhibit is due for a change soon. Will she know what it means? I can't really read the receipt. Is it a reproduction or found art of a real receipt?"

"She'll know."

"And what's the mistake?"

"Food poisoning," I say. The curator leans back and looks displeased. "Or medical mistake," I add.

"So the food poisoning is so bad it puts her in the hospital?"

"Yes," I say, glad that she's making it easy to fib on the spot.

"How much?" she asks.

I didn't expect a curator to be so blunt and capitalistic. I'm not sure what kind of number to ask for. Too high and she'll sour on me. Too low and she'll think I'm an amateur, and she'll never give me the information I need. I go all-in. "All I want is a name."

"What do you mean?" Rhea asks.

"The anonymous artist who created the statue, *Devin*. It's currently on display in—"

"Yes, I'm familiar with the piece," she says.

"So who made it?" I ask.

"Why?"

"I admire the work," I say, and it sounds convincing. "I want to meet the artist. As a fellow artist—"

"Excuse me," a light voice chirps from behind me. "Rhea Cieślak?"

"Yes," Rhea says.

"Am I interrupting? I thought we had a three o'clock meeting." The man wears a deeply stained smock and carries several tubes of rolled parchment.

I know I'm sunk, so I switch to a desperate version of *Option One*: "Just tell me. Please! Devin is my girlfriend. I need to know."

The curator slouches. She flicks the balled-up receipt onto the floor. "You're not the first to try," she says. "Even if you were an artist, I couldn't give you the name. Anonymous means anonymous. It'd be unethical."

Rhea doesn't look angry with me, and I'm glad. I hope my membership won't be revoked when Devin and I finally break up. I want to know about my future mistakes, I really do. I love the museum. I try to tell Rhea how important my museum membership is. "I love—"

Rhea interrupts. "I love you too," she says. Rhea touches my hand with her sticky fingers. "We all do. That's why you have an exhibit."

I turn and look at the artist who is nodding in agreement. "It's true. I love you too," he says.

"We can't do it without our patrons," Rhea adds. "You're so important to us." She is more understanding than the security guard. In this moment, I forget that I didn't get an answer. I'm still hopeless and lost, even as I smile and place my hand atop Rhea's. She rises from her chair, and I do too. Rhea hums while she walks me to the café door. She hands me her business card, and I'm on the next bus headed home.

———

On the back of Rhea's business card, there's a note. I didn't see her write it; it's like she already had this handwritten reminder prepared. It reiterates what she already told me: *Remember, even when you make mistakes, you are loved.*

I reread the card several times when I get home. It feels like a promise that my colossal mistake will be okay. The problem is, I'm not sure if I believe it.

"Do you love me?" I ask Devin, pocketing the business card.

She doesn't look up from her book. "What kind of stupid question is that? We say it all the time."

"I know, but do you mean it?"

"What?"

"It's just—" I consider how to explain it. "When you asked about lunch. How did you know I'd be near your work today?"

"I just assumed," she says. She dog-ears a page and puts the book on the nightstand. I hate it when she dog-ears books; it ruins the pages. Is that why we break up? Does she destroy all my books? I peer at what she's reading, and it looks like a library copy of some new sci-fi epic. Does the library ban her for dog-earing, and she goes nuts and takes her bookless frustration out on me?

I take a breath and refocus on the conversation at hand. "Why did you assume?" I ask.

"You're always at the museum on Mondays. You go there *all* the time."

"Exactly," I say. "You know me."

"Yeah, that's a good thing."

"But is that love, or does that only mean you're comfortable? Are you happy, or complacent?"

"What are you getting at? Are you unhappy?"

"No!" I shout. I take another breath. I think about last weekend: karaoke with friends; smiles and laughter; good sex when we got home; brunch the next day with my parents; work on Sunday at a good job—the kind that didn't hesitate to let me telecommute during the pandemic. My life is good. I feel happy. I am happy. "I'm not sure what I'm asking. Just ignore me."

"You were acting weird at lunch too. What's up?" Devin asks. She leans forward and touches my back. Her fingers curl around my ribs and pull me in for a hug.

"You think I was acting weird?" I ask. I know it's true, but the words sting, and I wonder if I've set the catastrophe in motion. I need a Xanax. I squirm beneath Devin's touch. I slide out and go to the bathroom to look for some pills.

Devin stands in the doorway and asks again, "What's up?"

"The museum," I say, popping a sleeping pill because I can't find anything else. "It had a statue of you."

"Okay, so?"

"Don't you get it? We're doomed. You're a mistake. I need to dump you," I say, and hearing the words aloud gives them new weight. I start to sweat.

"Do you want to dump me?" Devin asks.

"No," I say.

"And I don't want to dump you, so who cares about the statue?"

"The museum is never wrong," I remind her. "Remember that one time we thought it was wrong, and we went on that road trip to Bryce Canyon? Your car's engine basically blew up."

"You're being dramatic. It was just the radiator," Devin says.

"Still, it ended badly."

"It was fine. I had a good time," she says. "Besides, I've had a statue of you this whole time."

"What?"

"Before we even met. It was like a warning. I was trying to figure it out for weeks, then I met you at that cheese party thingy. I recognized you right away. I knew we wouldn't last."

"Holy shit! You had a statue of me?"

"Have. I still have it. It hasn't rotated out of my exhibit yet. It probably won't until we break up," she says. "I honestly thought you knew. When you visit the museum, do you *ever* go into my alcove? It's like two or three galleries away from yours."

I rarely look at any other art. I make a beeline for my area. I want to see my mistakes, but I don't care about the mistakes of others. When Devin visits the museum with me, she spends hours in all the showcases. She goes to the gift shop and picks out keychains and magnets featuring the mistakes of her friends, her brothers, her exes, her hairdresser—anyone and everyone. I usually get impatient and read a book in the museum lobby. Why have I never bothered to look at her exhibit? Perhaps my narcissism is what ends our relationship. Maybe this is the moment that she understands what a self-involved person I am.

Devin pulls out her phone and finds a picture. "See, here it is," she says. It's clearly from the same anonymous artist. The style is Grecian. Rather than looking skyward, my statue is in repose, a toga draped over the waist, oversized biceps contorted awkwardly around my face. It's beautiful, and it perfectly complements the *Devin* statue, like there's a different museum awaiting our joint exhibit—the Museum of Past Mistakes must exist somewhere.

Devin scrolls through photos of other prior exhibits, from before we met. There are artworks dedicated to other failed lovers, a gaudy lower back tattoo, and a job offer for a shitty company. They're all so intriguing—color-blocked modern art, vibrant primary colors, a suggestion of something rough and textural rippling beneath the paint. I can't wait to see her exhibit after I'm gone.

When the Astronauts Landed in Our Neighborhood

They touched down near the 7-Eleven, just off MLK and Sumner. Four of them, decked out in full spacesuits, large boots heavy in this new gravity, labored breathing moving through their suits like Darth Vader with asthma. They emerged from their spaceship to the tree-lined streets of Portland in an early December downpour. Rain hissed and evaporated as it pelted the hot spaceship exterior. Had they come six months earlier, they would've experienced that moment in June, just after the cold snaps, but long before wildfire smoke tinged the sky. A magical time when gentle spring sun gave way to street fairs, buskers, food trucks, and rosebuds brimming with promise.

Some neighbors tried to offer umbrellas, as was customary for welcoming strangers, even though the neighbors themselves thrived amid the rain—soaking into their skin, deep into cold ligaments and bone, strengthening their resolve as the clouded days shortened. However, the astronauts couldn't be bothered that first day, and they pushed past gathering crowds. They needed to build shelters before nightfall. They established base camp in the O'Reilly Auto Parts parking lot. They set up portable habitats and sensors on tripods and a recharging station for their rover.

On the second day, the astronauts left base camp as more rain clouds darkened the sky. They moved slowly around a four-block perimeter. They peered at dormant plant life and captured a pigeon. They inspected mailboxes and streetlamps, staring from behind their mirrored face shields, rain-streaked and beginning to fog. They were faceless and formless under these helmets, so alien-like, even though CNN reported that they had launched from the Kennedy Space Center in Florida several months earlier.

The neighborhood yet again took interest in this development. This time, the astronauts were more willing to engage as they wandered the area. They asked lots of questions. For example: *What do you call this place?* In response: *This is America.* The astronauts looked around, seemingly unsure, as if they had already visited America and knew this wasn't it. For another example: *How long have your people lived here?*

Eventually, the astronauts' daily explorations expanded indoors into the 7-Eleven. They inspected the shelves, picking up packages of Fritos and holding them beside some Funions for comparison. Having little money to purchase Fritos, Funions, or lotto tickets, the astronauts began asking for trades. They wanted to barter their freeze-dried rations and anti-gravity self-inking pens and spare bundles of wire and bolts and duct tape. In return, they wanted Krispy Kreme and hotdogs. They wanted glossy fashion magazines. They wanted Red Bull and cans of Starbucks Cold Brew.

Soon, the astronauts tired of the 7-Eleven, and they traded for more expensive items. They wanted to-go orders from some hip Alberta Street eateries. They wanted local art. They wanted televisions and stereo equipment. They cited all sorts of scientific reasons for these requests. For example: *We'd like to study the effects of sonic distortions of Lizzo's new album on your neighborhood's atmospheric properties.* For another example: *The chemical properties of a small batch craft IPA could lead to breakthroughs in understanding human metabolic functional variance.*

The astronauts got what they wanted because they were astronauts, and the neighborhood people knew that astronauts were admired and respected. The neighbors said emphatic things about the importance of this mission. For example: *I'm glad I can do my part! Astronauts are the last true heroes.* For another example: *Sure! Anything you need. Did you know that Buzz Aldrin spoke at my high school graduation back in the day?*

Though if anyone asked the neighbors in private, they'd admit they were thinking about more than civic duty. They were happy to get a souvenir from a bona fide NASA mission. They suspected that all these trades would be profitable. They went on eBay and OfferUp to see how much each collectable object might fetch them. In time, they learned that nobody cared about NASA trinkets unless it was something from the Apollo missions.

Trade relations soured. The astronauts went back to freeze-dried rations until they all began to complain. For example: *Fuck this shit.* Three of the astronauts took their little rechargeable rover into the rainy wastelands beyond their usual four-block perimeter. They sought other neighborhood frontiers, scouting for new sources of food and drink and culture and luxury and wealth—all for the sake of scientific cataloging, of course.

They left just one crew member to guard the skeletal remains of base camp, already low on supplies, tarps fraying in the cold breeze, power generator flickering more often than not. The lone astronaut deterred gawkers. For example: *Keep moving, shithead.* She chewed on her freeze-dried rations with contempt. She collected rainwater in buckets. She dug up a pile of weeds and burned them for heat. She dissected a raccoon and smeared its blood on her helmet. She threw bricks through the 7-Eleven's windows.

The astronaut waited nearly a week for her team to return, but they never did. She feared her fellow astronauts had been lost to the wilds just beyond Lombard Street. She informed ground control that the mission had been a failure. She told them that this planet was harsh and ruthless. For example: *It's a shithole. Needs terraforming. The next crew needs drills. Big ones.*

The astronaut initiated the launch sequence. She began her long, solitary journey into the cosmos, arcing deep into the cold void for months on end. Finally, she reached an apex, reversed thrusters, and plummeted down, down, down to a sunny Florida landing site where she was hailed a hero. She did a press circuit. She wrote a memoir.

She visited our neighborhood again to give a guest lecture at PCC's Cascade campus—this time, she came during the summertime. Her Delta Airlines flight touched down at the PDX airport with enough time for a quick in-and-out on her way to a more important stop in Los Angeles. She congratulated a scholarship recipient and said inspirational things. For example: *Young people are the future.* She shook hands with the college president. In her guest lecture, the astronaut told us all about her mission to Portland and everything that she learned about our neighborhood. For example:

Sharon's Lover is Dissipating

Sharon's lover is a smoke cloud. Or perhaps black mist is a better descriptor. He doesn't smell smoky, nor is he dry and suffocating. He is moist and dense, like a blackened fog. He hovers in the living room—barely moving, barely wafting—but Sharon remembers a time when his inky dew would dance and scatter across her body. She remembers how happy they once were.

They used to go to the symphony, and Sharon's lover would sneak away at intermission; he'd lodge his vaporous self in a tuba or trombone, escaping in thick plumes with each note, whispering a hidden melody to Sharon while other patrons gasped and murmured. They used to go to the movies, and her lover would drift to the projection box to make funny shadow puppets. They used to have picnics on the coast, and her lover would float above the waves, mixing with the salty breeze, dripping into the ocean and onto Sharon's skin like warm rain.

They had been carefree and foolish, and Sharon's lover lost part of himself after each outing—dissolved, evaporated, assimilated into a vast, distant atmosphere. Now there is less of him, and he seems unable to contain his remaining vapors. Sharon's lover is dissipating—even as he sits motionless above the sofa. He is too afraid to risk wafting around the tiny house, let alone a concert hall or movie theater or open ocean.

To save him, their life together must become insular. Sharon tells herself that any worthwhile relationship takes work. She begins telecommuting, and she equips every room with multiple fans. She sets up alternating barrages of humidifiers and dehumidifiers for perfect climate. These efforts are only temporary; Sharon's lover is still dissipating. He is leaking out of windows and under doors. Sharon plunges her hands into the middle of his densest vapors. His center is less tangible. She presses her hands together and shudders when her palms meet.

She hires a contractor to fortify and seal her house. The contractor warns that the modifications will be nearly airtight. It could be dangerous, he says. She agrees to pay double, and he shuts up.

As construction progresses, Sharon fights off headaches. Oxygen becomes a luxury item, ordered off eBay in heavy canisters—fifty bucks just for the goddamn shipping—and she gradually learns to need less and less of it.

While the contractor works, Sharon parades a series of shelter animals through the house—first birds, then cats, and finally dogs. One after another, the creatures gasp and wheeze and die. Like mineshaft canaries, each animal confirms dwindling oxygen levels and Sharon's increasing resilience. There are at least a dozen carcasses.

Soon, Sharon's lover will grow into a voluminous column of mist and smoke. He will fill the entire house, and they'll never be apart. She knows it. She looks forward to their new life together. She cancels all plans that require open doors and fresh air.

The contractor seals the porch last, turning it into an airlock. The contractor barely makes eye contact with Sharon. He takes clippings of cat and dog fur, and he smells the latent pet dander, and he weeps into his toolbox. He asks Sharon if he can take the last living dog—a gigantic mastiff, half-asleep and barely breathing. He rips up the entire bill and Sharon agrees.

    The contractor stumbles through the porch airlock. He falls onto the front yard and sucks air. He gasps and lets his lungs expand. Shrunken blood vessels in his appendages burst with renewed vigor, spilling red across Sharon's lawn. He wraps makeshift tourniquets around major arteries and pets the mastiff. He opens his lunchbox and feeds the dog half a bologna sandwich.

    Sharon finds the display sickening. She kicks aside the last eBay canister and vows to never use it. She puts blankets over the windows. She recedes into her living room, and she breathes deep, letting black vapors slide into her lungs.

Saw Act

I don't know how the saw act works. My assistant, Malvina, came up with it. It's not the usual cutting in half routine. We don't use a box with a foot-double curled in the base. In Malvina's saw act, she stands there, completely unobstructed and exposed. She stands, and I saw. It's one of those big old timey saws that sexy flannel-shirted lumberjacks use. There's nothing special about the saw at all. It grinds away. Blood splashes out. Malvina plops into two pieces. Her eyes roll back. Her intestines spill out. The air smells of rust. Then she winks at me with a milky, dead eye. The curtain drops for a couple seconds, concealing her from everybody, myself included. When the curtain rises again, she's perfectly fine. I extend my arms and flex my fingers, as if to indicate a rousing *Ta-da!* Sometimes I let a dove fly as the curtain rises—anything to make the crowd think I'm in charge.

The posters all bear my name: *Magesto the Magician*. I've been featured on *BuzzFeed*, hyped by influencers, booked for countless home-magic-kit-scam commercials, and profiled on *Atlas Obscura*'s main page as the most macabre act in Atlantic City—after that write-up, Malvina and I booked Vegas and never looked back. We do five shows a week. Three for the general public, two for high-roller VIPs. At each show, rain ponchos are distributed to the front row. The blood rarely sprays into the crowd, but it's a good marketing gimmick. I pull a salary unheard of on the strip. Each pay period, Malvina takes a fifty percent cut—also unheard of. I'm famous by all accounts. But I still don't know the goddamn saw act.

I test the lumberjack saw on dozens of other surfaces, hoping to figure it out. I saw through a bench. I cut a discarded tire in half. I cut down a palm tree on the strip. Tourists gather around and think it's performance art. I want them to leave me the fuck alone. I use the magician's secret weapon: misdirection. I encourage them to talk with a gaggle of nearby sex workers, and I keep sawing into anything I can. I drape curtains over these halved items, yank them off for a big reveal, but nothing happens.

I give up and decide to plead with Malvina directly—I've never let her know how much it bothers me before. She had trusted my routines without a single question. Even the dangerous ones—like the inferno act that we did in Jersey—I gave her written instructions, she nodded, and that was it. I do my routines, and she does hers. The saw act has been her staple since she signed on. She insisted on it during the interview. She showed videos of her rehearsals. She said she'd perfected it since childhood, sawing toads in half with her sister.

I get down on one knee. Malvina arches her eyebrow at my posture, possibly mistaking this moment for some unexpected and unwanted proposal. "Please, tell me how to do the saw act," I say.

"It's my only trick. Just let me have this one. We make a good team, don't we?" she says, sliding out of her bedazzled costume and donning a hoodie.

"But it's driving me crazy. I need to know."

"It doesn't matter," Malvina says. "We're killing it out there." She pulls back the curtain, and I hear a wave of murmurs like *Fantastic!* and *How did he do it?* and *Oh my gawd, I need to Instagram this.*

"But I'm the magician. It's my act," I say.

"Just keep doing your hat tricks and that levitation thing. Leave the saw act to me," she says. She pulls the hoodie down and obscures her face. I hear her sniffling underneath. I'm not sure if she's crying or getting a cold or allergies. Regardless, she's done listening to my groveling. She disappears into the bright Vegas night.

On payday, I spend half my earnings on the strip. I go to the lounge where I met my most recent boyfriend—the one who turned out to be a coke mule. I buy everybody a drink, but I abstain. I don't drink anymore. Still, buying rounds gives a similar sense of barroom belonging and euphoria.

I bum a cigar off a guy and blow smoke rings. I tell the guy I'm a magician. I hope he will be impressed and go home with me. His cheap suit tells me he's not a regular in the lounge, and maybe he's looking for a Vegas night to remember.

"What, like card tricks?" he asks.

"No, not like card tricks," I say. I pull out my phone and swipe through pictures of the performance.

"That's sick, dude. All that blood. Gross," he says. He puts out his cigar and makes his way to the slots.

A woman in a sequin leotard comes over. I recognize her. I think she used to be in Cirque du Soleil. The leotard she's in looks secondhand, so she's probably in a worse show now. "You're Magesto, right?" she says.

"Yeah," I say.

"What's your real name?" she asks, knocking back a shot.

"Magesto. I had it legally changed," I say. I hate the name now—it sounds like the name of a pimply teenage magician who does coin tricks—but it's been trademarked and marketed, so there's no going back.

She laughs and touches my arm. Maybe I will hook up with somebody tonight. "You're a fraud, right?" she says, digging her glittered nails into my skin.

"What? No. I mean, to the extent that every magician is playing tricks on people, then sure, but—"

She cuts me off. "You know what I mean. You don't know how to do the trick, do you?"

"What trick?" I ask, but I know she means the saw act.

She scoffs and releases my arm. "Whatever. It's okay. I'm a fraud too," she says with a smile. I'm not entirely sure what she means, but I'm glad she's off the saw act topic. She holds up her empty shot glass. She wants a refill. I mostly ignore her even as she applies a fresh coat of cherry red lipstick and makes a perfect pout.

I consider whether Malvina is telling people. She could be shopping around her resume, boasting the saw act as her signature trick. She's marketable as a solo headliner—it wouldn't matter that she only does one trick. Without her, I'd be nothing. "I have to go," I say, but the former Cirque du Soleil performer isn't paying attention at this point. She's clutching somebody else's arm with that sharp grip. I drop some cash on the bar so she can get another shot, and I follow my first target out to the slots. His cheap suit looks even more like polyester in the neon slot machine lights. I want him to smile at me and put on cherry red lipstick. Instead, he frowns and leaves as I approach.

The machine is hot, so I play a few. I win a little, and I play another few. A waitress gives me three gin and tonics on the house, and I distribute them to nearby gamblers. The only guy who will make eye contact has a wife. The only woman who seems interested seems too wholesome for my bedroom proclivities—she's got pearls and a dress that might as well be a painter's smock—I doubt she's ever seen a strap-on let alone worn one. Maybe I'm wrong, but I don't want to put in the effort to find out, so I go back to my room alone.

As I make my way to the elevator, I pass the lounge. The woman with the red lipstick and sharp nails is half-shouting and half-slurring something unintelligible. Security politely asks her to get the fuck out.

Back in my room, I pull my Russian nesting dolls from the display shelf. Each doll has a different face; there's a stoic exterior doll, but different emotions cascade through the doll's core. The vendor told me this is more authentic, like how Russian dolls used to be made, back before mass production. I don't know if that's true, but I like the symbolism of a hard exterior with a more nuanced interior. I think about Malvina, and I consider her interior faces. I don't know if I've ever seen her smile off-stage. But she's got a great on-stage smile—toothy and instantly joyous. I open and close the dolls in sequence a few times. The repetitive action helps me wind down and relax before falling onto the pillow top.

I wake earlier than usual. Rehearsal is several hours away. I hit up the omelet bar and ask for absolutely everything. The lumpy omelet is equally sweet and spicy but surprisingly not bad. I have some emails from my manager, Al, but the subject lines don't seem important. I move a serrated knife across my skin—lightly at first, then hard enough to make tiny white scrapes that don't quite bleed. For a moment, I think I'm onto something, then I draw blood and ruin the last of my omelet. I suck down coffee dregs and leave a good tip.

I arrive to rehearsal early—partly because I want to apologize to Malvina for begging her to reveal her secret—but also partly because I don't have shit to do today. Although, I suppose that's not unusual. I rarely have shit to do other than sulk. Sometimes I call my brothers just to rub my success in their faces. Sometimes I gamble. Sometimes I look up sex dolls online. Sometimes I look into Russian brides and Russian husbands and Russian circuses who may need a magician. Then I look up information on therapists and whether being obsessed with a place you've never been to is a syndrome or disorder or nothing. Turns out it's nothing. But besides all that shit, I don't have anything to do today.

The lights are on when I arrive. Malvina is already there. It's an hour before our scheduled meet, and I realize that I typically arrive late rather than early. She's on the otherwise empty stage. She's holding a whirring buzzsaw near her torso. The saw is shiny and new, price tag still attached. I don't think she's seen me yet, so I crouch down in the back row. This is my chance to see how the trick works. She holds the saw inches from her body. She is wailing even though it hasn't pierced her skin yet. She drops the saw before making contact. The buzzsaw skids across the stage and chomps into plank flooring. Malvina starts sobbing.

"I know you're there," she says. I pretend to tie my shoe as a feeble explanation for why I'm crouched. "So you're spying on me now?" she asks.

"Are you working on something new?" I counter.

"No," she says.

"What about the old saw?" I say, motioning to the lumberjack saw propped against a chair just off stage.

"That's still what we'll use," she says. She walks over to the buzzsaw and pulls it from the stage, wood cracking as she dislodges it. "This is nothing. Don't worry about it."

"It doesn't look like nothing."

"It is," she insists. She puts the buzzsaw in a large clamshell case. It's been decked out with rhinestones. I know a magician's traveling kit when I see one.

I decide to go for it, blunt and honest: "Are you going solo?"

"No," she says. "How could you think that? After all we've been through."

"What have we been through?" I ask. I'm not trying to be a jackass. I truly can't think of anything significant.

"You're an asshole," she says. "I moved here for this. I moved here for the show. It's not just the money. This is my art too."

"It's not art. And you moved here from Jersey. Big fucking deal," I say, and I regret it instantly.

"You're on your own tonight," she says.

Since I've already fucked myself over—and apparently I like fucking myself over—I decide to prod once more: "Do you have something else booked? Are you with that Cirque du Soleil girl?"

Malvina shakes her head. "What the fuck are you talking about? Cirque du Soleil? Do you want to know what this electric saw is for?"

"Yeah, enlighten me," I say, and it sounds even more sarcastic than it is.

"It was for you, dumbass." She disappears with a puff of smoke, probably into the trapdoor beneath the stage. It seems like a waste of special effects. I reload the smoke cannon. I prep the rest of my instruments and check the rigging. I wait backstage for hours because I have nowhere else to go. I lay flat on my back while the stagehands walk around me and avoid eye contact. Al tries calling, but I do not answer.

That night, I perform solo for the first time in years. I do my usual hat tricks. I make an audience member disappear from a small on-stage closet. I levitate. But I do not cut anything in half. Rain ponchos rustle impatiently in the front row. Somebody is writing in a small black notebook. She looks like a reviewer. Her clutch is red. Reviewers like red. She's probably got a red sports car too.

I buy drinks for everybody at the bar again. I pity their burgeoning hangovers in one of the world's brightest cities. I smoke another cigar. I demand a pizza with everything on it, even though the cook says it'll be soggy from all the toppings—and he's right. I lose some blackjack.

I finally check Al's voicemail. His message is panicked. "Malvina quit," he shouts. "We're fucking sunk. Without her, the act is nothing. What did you say to her? What did you do? She was our golden goose, you fucking idiot. You better have a new trick to debut for tomorrow's VIPs. It needs to be spectacular. You need a replacement for the saw act. If you can't deliver, your penthouse and fat salary are gone. You fucking hear me? And pick up the damn phone next time I call." The robotic voicemail menu asks if I want to replay or delete, and I scream obscenities at the robo-menu as if Al can hear it.

I call a car and head to the nearest hardware store to inspect the merchandise. I look at rows of sinister blades. I never knew there were so many types, each with different tooth patterns, each purporting the ability to cut various materials: wood, metal, concrete. A clerk asks, "Can I help you?"

"Which one is best for human flesh?" I ask. I don't expect an answer, but the clerk offers one. His recommendation doesn't look as hefty as the buzzsaw that Malvina was testing. I can't decide if a smaller saw will be easier or harder. Either way, I'm ready to see how this trick works.

Kitten Egg

My cat lays an egg. What the hell, cat?
    I'm not sure what to do with the aforementioned egg. My cat doesn't seem to know either. She bats it around. I worry that she will break it, so I put the egg in my bathroom and close the door. I text my boyfriend about the cat egg. He says he's not in the mood for jokes.
    I google some egg stuff. I read that a forty-watt bulb will keep the egg warm. I only have LED light bulbs, and I'm not sure if I should look at the actual wattage or the incandescent equivalent. Why are there no good websites about post-Edison egg hatchery? I decide that a warm blanket is good enough.
    My cat sits outside the bathroom door meowing. It's that low-pitched meow that she does whenever she wants to pounce. I fear for the egg, but it's not really my problem, so I go to bed.
    By morning, the bathroom door is open, the egg is bigger, and my cat is gone. I put up Lost Cat signs, but I suspect she was absorbed into the egg. I take the door off its hinges and roll the egg out of the bathroom. I arrange some blankets on the living room floor and watch TV with the egg. I pet the egg as if it were my cat. It vibrates a little, like soundless purring. I call my boyfriend and tell him about this latest development. I say he should come over and see for himself. He's drinking with his buddies and can't make it.

I fall asleep on my sofa. By morning, the egg is regular sized, and my boyfriend stops by with coffee.

He doesn't believe that the egg was ever huge or that it absorbed my cat. He says we should stop bickering and start looking for my cat.

I say I already put up Lost Cat signs.

He says that I'm in denial.

I say I'm not.

He says that the egg is bullshit and that I'm delusional.

I say he's an asshole, and I know he's screwing his ex.

He says he's not, and he accuses me of calling phone sex lines.

I say I'm not, even though I really am. It's embarrassing. Who actually calls one-nine-hundred numbers these days? It's all about the Internet and webcams now, but for some reason sound gets me off more than sight.

He threatens to break the egg but storms out instead.

As he leaves, my cat saunters past him, back into the apartment. My boyfriend shakes his head at the cat.

My cat sits on the egg gently.

Hospital Story

You are in a hospital waiting room. There is a rack of magazines nobody wants to read. There are chairs. These chairs are old and have a scratchy burlap-like consistency. Or maybe they're plastic—newer hospitals typically have plastic chairs. Either way, the chairs are always uncomfortable—this is true of all hospitals.

Hospital stories always have a sick person by default. You do not feel sick. And you are in the waiting room, and there's a nurse avoiding eye contact because somebody you love must be dying, and she knows it, and the doctors all know it, but they cannot say for sure until a litany of tests are performed. On television, paramedics always use defibrillator paddles on long-dead corpses, like they need to go through the motions.

You tear off a piece of a magazine. *Time* or *People* or *Sports Illustrated*. Maybe there's a copy of *Highlights*, but that seems more like a dentist's office thing—you could complete the maze with a gigantic magic marker and show all the kids how smart you are. This particular torn-out magazine page talks about celebrity gossip. Or perhaps it talks about a new beauty trend. It talks about fine lines. It talks about pores. You don't understand pores. At the spa, they always talk about opening your pores. In television commercials for expensive creams, they always talk about closing pores—shrinking, minimizing. Contradictions like these beget wars. Spa attendants dump boiling massage oil down the murder hole. Estheticians fight back with makeshift paraffin flamethrowers. In this wartime article, there is a picture of a flagellating monk with flawless pores—*macro*dermabrasion. A before-and-after is blown up to 10x magnification, moon craters on one side and nubile skin on the other.

You ball up the torn-out article and toss it toward a nearby wastebasket. It misses. A *Sports Illustrated* tear-out might hit the mark. Your biceps swell at the thought of exercise—a body in motion. You feel vigorous in this hospital. Your heartbeat clangs like cymbals, mocking the defibrillator paddles.

Despite the illusory gravitas in your veins, real displays of fitness are few and far between. The last time you played a sport was two or three years ago. Basketball, with your nephews. You had twisted your ankle and ended up in a doctor's office. Office visits are lighthearted stories. They feature morality tales and bildungsromans and aforementioned twisted ankles. But this is not an office visit. This is a hospital. Hospital visits are fundamentally bleak.

There are other people in the waiting room, each busying themselves with magazines or panicked cell phone conversations or crying or bleeding through bandages or coughing. This looks more like a triage center than a waiting room. Everybody keeps to their own increasingly shrinking zones. Uncomfortable chairs fill at unpredicted speed.

A man sits next to you. You know that protocol dictates a polite smile, but no other pleasantries will be exchanged. Hospital waiting rooms are places of privacy and mutual solemnity.

The man digs in his pants and pulls out a pocketknife. You want him to slice off his earlobe and present it to you. Instead, he opens the pocketknife's corkscrew attachment and retrieves a bottle of wine from deep within his backpack. Hospital stories are sometimes about toasts and celebration—like newborn babies. Or maybe alcoholism.

You dig in your coat and hope to find a pocketknife because there's something romantic about carrying a pocketknife. Instead, there are crumbled Ritz crackers and a safety pin and three pennies and a balled-up piece of paper. You decide that this paper must be a *Sports Illustrated* page, self-torn and migrated from a nearby magazine. You shoot for the wastebasket again. You miss.

A doctor whispers to the nurse who breaks her no-eye-contact rule. They both stare at you. You know what this is about. This is a hospital story. Somebody has died. This has been the obvious plot since before the magazine or the pocketknife.

The deceased individual is somebody close to you because this is a hospital story. It's either Mom or Dad or Brother or Sister. Maybe it's Uncle, but only if the twist ending is that he molested you, and the tender grief-stricken narrative disintegrates into a different type of hospital story. You view Uncle's lifeless body, and it is cathartic, or maybe it's anticlimactic because his death doesn't undo the past.

Or it could be a baby. Or alcoholism. Or pills. It could be that Aunt is a drug addict with an elevated heart rate and blood in her stool and withdrawal and stolen Blu-ray players and sucking off the doctor for oxycodone scripts. Or maybe it's meth. Why do tweekers on television always have uncharacteristically good teeth? But it's probably Mom or Dad or Brother or Sister. It's cancer. It must be. That's what most hospital stories are about. The big C.

The doctor and nurse read the chart in tandem like it's a public declaration. You leave mid-pronouncement. Because this is a hospital story, but it isn't yours.

Delilah

My neighbor, Pete, has been my main human contact during the COVID-19 lockdowns. We chat from our respective backyards. It's outdoors, and there's a fence between us, so I think it's safe and within CDC guidelines. I look forward to these backyard social visits amid a week of constant Zoom, emails, and anxiety over recent workplace budget cuts.

Before the coronavirus, we only talked once a month—usually at a barbeque or a movie night with friends. Now, it's daily. Overall, I'm grateful for this minor semblance of a social life. But lately, I'm getting sick of his constant hair talk. He's obsessed with how long his hair has grown during lockdown. The last few times we talked, he reminded me that he wants to change his name to Sam, short for Samson.

While it's obnoxious, I must admit the selfies he sent look impressive—at first, I thought they were Photoshopped. He has long, brown curls draped past his shoulders—much longer than I thought possible with a couple months of growth.

"I'm telling you, let it grow," he says from behind the cedar fence. "It gives you strength. Like Samson."

"I'm not religious," I say.

"Neither am I. But long hair is a symbol in lots of cultures," Pete says.

"So what's your point?" I ask.

"All our power is in our hair. You just need to know how to use it."

"I've had long hair before. It didn't make me stronger," I say. I don't add the part about hating long hair. My chin-length bob is enough for now. As soon as lockdown ends and salons reopen, I'm getting it all chopped off. I usually prefer something close to a pixie cut.

"That's what they want you to think."

"Who?"

"I don't know. Philistines?" Pete says.

"You're nuts," I say.

"Maybe. But check this out." A loud crunch echoes from Pete's yard. A metal snow shovel, bent and curled into a pile of scrap, arcs over the fence and craters into the dirt near my toolshed.

I haven't left the neighborhood in a long time. I joke that I might forget how to drive. I order delivery more often than I used to. I want to support local restaurants, otherwise they'll all vanish before this is over. I get all my groceries curbside. I don't need much else to survive. But surviving is one thing, coping is another.

I want to go on a long walk. No specific destination, just a walk deep into the city to discover something. Maybe a bookstore. An out-of-the-way boutique. Drinks with a dashing stranger. Or even drinks by myself sounds nice. Dinner for one at an upscale restaurant. It's not even about the socialization at this point. It's about the space—the air—the ability to move around. Yeah, I could go on a walk with a mask, but I'd feel guilty. It's frivolous, and I try to follow public health guidance—and right now, the more I limit my movement and possible contacts, the better. If we all shelter-in-place, we'll get through this.

Pete leaves constantly these days. The first couple months, he stayed inside. Now, with his long hair, he's fearless—or perhaps just reckless. I ignore it at first, but then he starts bringing people home. I hear them in the backyard, moaning as they rub against one another.

Some might be Grindr or Tinder hookups, but I strongly suspect many of these men and women are sex workers. On some level, I'm glad they're getting work. This recession hurts us all, and sex workers can't get unemployment benefits. But I also can't get past the complete disregard for COVID-19 precautions. When Pete is finally alone in the backyard, I tell him, "You're gonna get sick. Or spread it to somebody else as a carrier."

"Because they're prostitutes? They're usually wearing masks. And you can't get it through sex. You're just a prude."

"No. I'm not a prude. I'm just safe. Why do you think I do contactless drop-off for everything? You can't have contactless sex." I touch the misshapen snow shovel. The sun has been beating on the metal, and it almost burns my hand.

"It's not even about the sex," Pete says. I only half-believe him since I've heard them fucking. I'm sure the whole neighborhood has heard it. "I need somebody to look at me like she used to."

"Who? Your ex? What was her name—Maggie, right?"

"No, not Maggie. I'm talking about Delilah," Pete says. "She's everything. Even though she betrayed me over and over."

"Pete, I'm worried about you," I say.

"I have them tie me up," Pete says in response to a question I never asked. "I break free every time. I punish them for their treachery. They call me Sam. I call them Delilah. It's really hot, but it's not the same. None of them even try to cut my hair."

"I think you need to talk to somebody else about this. We're all going through some tough shit right now. Maybe you can find a telehealth therapist in your insurance network. I've been seeing one every other week for anxiety. It helps."

"Whatever," Pete says.

"Seriously, Pete—" I begin, but he cuts me off.

"My name is Sam!" he screams. The fence buckles. Concrete piers teeter. A post tumbles over. A cloud of dirt and dust obscures my vision. I cough and try to make sense of the chaos. The rest of the fence falls, and there's a tremendous *crack* and *smash*. Hair engulfs me, blotting out the sunlight.

The dust wafts away. Pete hovers over me—way closer than the CDC-recommended six feet. I feel the warmth of his breath. His eyes are bloodshot. He's gripping an entire ten-foot fence post. He throws it aside, and it lands with a thud. He recedes into his otherworldly hair—dense, flowing even with no breeze, almost like an opaque liquid. He steps back into his yard.

"Sorry," Pete says. I don't reply. He continues to explain himself. "I didn't mean to get so close. But don't worry. I'm immune to COVID. I'm strong. I'm invincible against everything except Delilah. She's my weakness." He goes back inside, and I brush dust and cedar splinters off my clothes. Luckily, I don't think I'm bleeding. The fence seems to have missed me—or maybe Pete shielded me from the worst of it.

I haven't gone back outside since Pete ripped apart the fence. At our usual meeting time, Pete strolls between both yards with impunity, pacing back and forth, waiting for me. His hair moves less now, like it has lost some energy. I can't see his face. He hunches over and the hair consumes him. The crushed shovel and shattered fence are joined by other objects. Pete compresses his trash cans into wads of metal. He rips the roof off my toolshed. He rolls a boulder into the yard and pummels it into clay. Day after day, he shows me his strength.

  He grunts and screams so loud that my windows rattle. He's coughing regularly, and he spits blood into my birdbath. He acts so feral, but then he retreats to his house at sunset, and I swear his hair shrinks a little as he ducks inside. He calls, and we talk at night, just like we used to in the backyard. He's lucid, and we share gripes about slow Internet, dwindling toilet paper reserves, and how we miss hugging our friends. He still hasn't apologized for the fence, and I've stopped asking him to. I mention the cough and the blood. Pete claims he's already taken a COVID test, but I don't believe him.

  In these phone calls, he sounds scared and anxious, his thunderous cough stifled to a wheeze as he tells me about binging *The Great British Bake Off*. But every morning, he becomes a raging beast in my backyard again. Sometimes, he frightens me. Other times, I want to be like him. I browse speed bags on Amazon and watch MMA clips on YouTube. I wonder if it's possible to bend steel without growing my hair.

Pete calls me a few minutes after he destroys the fire hydrant—I worry that some houses on our block will have basement flooding. I think about sending it to voicemail—it's daytime and he might not be lucid—but he's still my friend.

  "I've been reading," Pete says, his voice hoarse.

  "That's good," I say. "I'm glad you're focusing on something else. You know I worry about—"

  "Did you know there's more about Samson than the hair?" I want to hang up, but I don't. "Everybody knows he had long hair and was strong. But he was also smart. Wise. He was a judge."

"A judge? Like in a court?"

"He ruled over people. He was basically an early version of a king. And he told this riddle one time, about bees and honey and a lion."

"A lion? What's the punchline. I don't—"

"There's no punchline. It's a riddle, not a joke," Pete coughs, and it sounds wet—I worry he's got liquid in his lungs. "But yeah, there's a lion involved. He ripped one apart with his bare hands. Also, did you know he killed an entire army with the jawbone of a donkey?"

"A donkey jawbone? A mutilated lion? This guy's a psycho. Animal abuse is an early sign of a serial killer, you know." I chuckle a little, but it's not funny, and I know I'm testing Pete's ability to stay calm.

"I don't want to be a psycho," Pete says, and he's serious, his voice soft underneath the strain.

"I don't mean it like that—"

"I'm scared," he says.

I'm not sure how to respond. I want to let him know that I understand—or at least I think I understand. My toes chill. My carpet is saturated. The hydrant rupture must've been bad. Pete probably ripped apart some of the underground water mains during his rampage. I make my way across the squishy floor and look outside. There's a thick sludge of water and something brown frothing across the street. I hope it's mud and not sewage.

"I feel like I need to destroy things," Pete says. "Like I have this urge to break everything around me. Like something or someone is telling me to do it. Is that God, do you think? Is God telling me to break shit?" He coughs harder. I hear him spit in the background.

"I don't know. If it is, then God's pretty messed up," I say. Sirens wail in the distance. I'm not sure who else is aware of Pete's strength. I wonder if the neighbors will rat him out to the cops.

There's a sniffle on the other end of the line. I think Pete's crying. "I have this strength, but I have nothing to do with it. It just smolders there. It's like—" he trails off into a long silence.

"Pete? Are you still there?" I ask. There's no response. "Sam?"

"Will you be my Delilah?" he asks.

"Yes," I say without hesitation. Scissors alone won't be enough. I'll shave every follicle down to the scalp.

My Fingernails Are Haunted

I get weekly manicures with thick, armor-like nail polish. Gel finish. It requires a special machine to cure the chemicals. These measures keep the ghost happy most of the time. We have a delicate homeostasis. The ghost moans when I do quarterly reports—tap, tap, tapping on the keyboard in near-rhythmic fashion. Beyond that, we coexist just fine.

Daytime is my time. It's an unspoken rule. But at night, the ghost is free to be a ghost. I brush my teeth and wash off my makeup, and the lights flicker. The ghost can't manipulate the environment very well. Just small electrical flashes like that. I wonder if that's common for ghosts. Maybe other ghosts can fling chairs across the room like in movies—but those ghosts probably take up residence in pumping hearts, throbbing frontal lobes, the eyes of rabid dogs, the lungs of serial killers breathing free. I don't think the best ghosts wind up in fingernails.

I crawl into bed, and the ghost tells me all its sinister, haunting, ghostly things. "Mak is gonna leave you for that hot girl in accounting. Your ass looks flat in those new jeans. There's nothing but sadness after you die. You'll wind up in somebody's fingernails or toenails or eyelashes. You'll hate it. Your mother doesn't love you. And you're going to die soon. I smell the stink on you. Bone cancer. Yes, it's bone cancer. Only a matter of time. No doctor can save you. Also, your crow's feet are getting worse. And your dad lied to you. He didn't know what it's like to be haunted. But did you know that Linh is haunted? I can tell when another ghost is nearby. Linh's ghost is going to kill her too. Everybody you love is going to die."

It's always like this. My fingernails writhe underneath my blanket—so do my legs, but I think that's undiagnosed restless leg syndrome.

The ghost tires itself out, I get some sleep, and we both repeat the cycle.

My first tooth came in on a Friday, and I started biting my nails on Saturday. That's what Mom told me.

My earliest childhood memories involve hospital rooms. I chewed past the quick and kept going. I needed sutures on several digits. My nails were sickly and dying—prime real estate for a ghost.

"You brought this on yourself. Biting your nails is such a nasty habit. You'll always get a ghost if you do such nasty things. Cigarettes too," Mom declared.

But I wasn't so sure. Classic chicken-or-egg scenario. Yeah, maybe it was my fault, but I also wondered if my nails were haunted since birth. Maybe I heard the ghost whispering sweet somethings, and it freaked me out, so I chewed to make the voices stop.

One birthday, when I was seven or eight, Mom gave me delicate handmade gloves to hide my wounds. I bled through the gloves, and the ghost in my fingernails laughed.

My boss wants me to input data from some bullshit SWOT survey, so today is a heftier typing load than usual, and my ghost is annoyed. It's not as bad as the quarterlies, but still not great. Our homeostasis is briefly out-of-whack. I apologize to the ghost. The ghost says, "It's okay. Not your fault. But also, you'll die at this dead-end job. And nobody likes you. Mak is definitely fucking her. Your breath is terrible."

I open my desk drawer and retrieve my emergency gloves—thick as oven mitts. "Shhh," I hush the ghost, and I take a break from typing. I chew some gum in case the ghost is right about my breath.

I make out with Mak in the break room, and I ask, "Do you like that hot girl from accounting?"

"Which one? They're all hot in accounting," Mak says with a laugh.

I'm not laughing. Mak's face turns red with embarrassment. I think the ghost's taunt might be true. It's usually a toss-up—my ghost makes up shit just to provoke me, but it also stumbles onto truth sometimes. Like that time it said Dad would not survive his heart attack. I break the silence: "You know I'm talking about Cynthia. She's the hottest one."

"Oh, is she? I didn't notice," xe says.

Laughter comes from my left pinky, muffled by my emergency gloves. Mak responds with a chuckle of xir own.

"Fuck you," the ghost screams. I'm not sure if it's directed at me or Mak.

The ghost was the worst when I was a teenager. The ghost told me I was gonna die during my driver's ed test, and I got nervous and fucked up the parallel parking. The ghost shouted obscenities in geometry class and got me detention. In study hall, the ghost told everyone at school that I gave blowjobs to donkeys and ate raw chicken for dinner. I chewed my fingers until only a sliver of nail remained, but the taunts never stopped.

I got a part-time job at Walgreens and tried a new approach. I purchased and/or shoplifted things that might soothe the ghost in my fingernails—lotions, nail polish, a bubbly hand-massager contraption filled with Epsom salts. These early gifts were the start of our semi-peaceful coexistence. The ghost calmed. My fingers healed. I traded my nail-biting habit for cigarettes, and Mom shook her head. I went to college.

I inspect my nails in the bathroom. Some of my extra-thick gel polish has chipped. Normally, I'd wait until the weekend, but today's typing marathon must've caused tiny fractures. The ghost won't calm down until I get this fixed. I can expect more small outbursts—laughter, hissing, snarling, a curse word bellowed in the middle of the cubicles.

I duck out for a manicure. At the nail salon, the ghost shrieks a couple times as the old polish is removed, but it soon relaxes. With Linh's blend of hydrating oils, gentle exfoliants, and precision cuticle removal, my ghost settles into a low hum—almost like a purring cat.

I tip fifty percent. I always do. Linh is so patient when it comes to my ghost.

I return to work just before closing and gather my things. I pass Cynthia in the parking lot, and I ask her out on a date.

The call center was my first full-time job. I never had real insurance before. I used all my medical leave the moment it accrued, checking for all the ailments the ghost had ever mentioned.

Tuberculosis. Tetanus. Hepatitis. Congestive heart failure. Most often, the ghost told me I had bone cancer. Part of me knew that the ghost was just trying to scare me—that's what ghosts do. But another part of me was convinced. The ghost insisted, "The cancer is calling to me. I'm a ghost. I know this shit. I know when people are dying. You're gonna be a ghost soon. Just like me. You'll haunt that poor doctor after she gives you a terminal diagnosis. You're dying right now. Yes. Dying. I can smell it."

The doctor ran every test and found no evidence of anything, including bone cancer. She prescribed Lorazepam for anxiety.

I googled "bone cancer" and learned it's extremely rare. I learned that when people talk about bone cancer, they actually mean a different cancer has spread. Cancer rarely starts in the bones. But once it reaches to the bones, it's particularly deadly and incurable—burrowed so deep into your core that it undermines the most solid, seemingly indestructible parts of you. Your bones. Your fingernails too.

"Ghosts are a normal part of growing up," Dad assured me. "I've got at least ten of my own. Ghosts are everywhere, but you don't realize it until you're an adult with a mortgage."

We always lived in apartments, so I wasn't sure how a mortgage was relevant.

"You'll see. Now that you've got a college degree and a full-time job, you'll get even more ghosts. They ain't that bad," Dad said. I appreciated the sentiment, but I didn't think Dad really understood a true haunting.

Haunted people aren't smiling all the time.

Haunted people don't kiss their wife and kid goodbye before a six-week long haul and return home looking well-rested.

Haunted people are tormented and empty, and ghosts take advantage, filling that space with their malevolence.

Dad always seemed full. Brimming with the opposite of a ghost.

In bed, lights out, I expect the ghost to tell me more about my doomed relationship, or how my Mom is disappointed in me, or how I'm not gonna get the promotion I want, or how I'm gonna die some grisly death any moment. Even in our typical homeostasis, the ghost always takes advantage of darkness, unfettered and boisterous.

There's a prolonged silence. The ghost must be too comfortable in its new, cozy layer of gel polish.

"Are you there?" I ask.

"Yeah," the ghost says.

"Okay, just checking," I say.

"You're gonna die," the ghost says, but it sounds forced. The alarm clock on my nightstand blinks "6:66" for a moment. It's an old trick, like the flickering lights. The ghost still can't do much beyond these blips. I feel sorry for the ghost. It probably wants more from its afterlife—cracking a house's foundation, lighting unholy fires, impaling paranormal investigators who dare challenge it.

"Tell me again," I say. "When am I gonna die?"

"Any minute now," the ghost says. "There's cancer growing in your stomach. I can smell it."

"I thought it was bone cancer?"

"Yes, that's right. Also, your brain. There's a fat, juicy tumor in your brain."

"Okay. Sounds good. Thanks for the update," I say.

"Are you scared yet?" the ghost asks.

"Yes," I say in the darkness. "Terrified." I grasp my comforter and pull it close. I kiss my haunted fingernails goodnight.

The Gull Bone Index

We've been freefalling for months according to Becky's day planner. An expanse of mountainous crags stretches beneath us, endless and unmoving. Perspective lines do not shift. Daniel insists we move closer to the ground each day—he has developed a method of squinting and measuring distances with his fingers.

The rush of constant velocity had been nauseating at first, but Becky and Daniel adapted within days. I still vomit some mornings. I dream about falling, and I wake just before I hit the ground, but then I'm still falling in real life, and it's a giant mindfuck of contradictory sensations. I'm weightless and seemingly motionless, but I know there's violent gravity at work. The law of attraction—that's what Becky's textbook calls it. We take turns reading to pass the time. Her backpack contents are the only sources of amusement we have.

We spend the morning riding jet streams away from our waste and my occasional vomit, which falls next to us at a constant speed. Becky's textbook talks about a hammer and feather and how they'd each fall at the same rate in a vacuum.

We spend the afternoon trapping birds. A flock approaches and we ready our small net, stitched together from socks, shoelaces, and whatever clothing could be spared. We catch a gull. Becky plucks the feathers and stuffs them in her purse. She has trouble sleeping without a pillow and almost has enough feathers for a facsimile. I worry that the purse-pillow will drift away in the middle of the night.

Daniel cleans a bone and announces that he's fine-tuning a new method for measuring our descent. He holds the bone in front of his eye and does that same tired squint. He maps approaching cloud formations. I've never seen him interested in the clouds before—maybe the unchanging ground has gotten boring. "Eight-hundred-nineteen-point-two gull bone indexed latitude," he says, as if that means anything.

Becky spies a shattered piece of airplane fuselage falling in the distance. She tells me how her niece builds model planes. She says it's her niece's birthday tomorrow, double-checking her day planner to be certain. I say we should celebrate. She agrees. We rummage through Becky's backpack of goodies and find some old receipts. We tear off little nubs of paper and toss them like confetti. The papery snow hovers all around us. We approach Daniel's eight-hundred-nineteen-point-two cloud. It rises like a fluffy continent beneath us.

We enter the cloud, and in the zero-visibility haze, we frantically shout "Marco" and "Polo" to each other, desperate and hopeful and terrified between each call-and-response.

Evolution of Apartments

328 square foot studio, all utilities included. Live on a futon. Eat noodles from dehydrated packets. Take cold showers. Make a zine. Burn something. Say something profound and jot it in a notebook so that years from now you can realize how pretentious and naïve you once were.

410 square foot one-bedroom in an old house, long ago quartered into rickety standalone units. Live at your desk. Microwave vegetarian burritos. Get an outdoor cat. Think about grad school. Hallucinate miniature sharks pouring from the bathroom sink. Rip out the plumbing and forfeit your security deposit.

905 square foot two-bedroom in a swanky high-rise, priced beyond your comfort zone. Live off credit cards. Read a cookbook and make dinners from scratch. Get an indoor cat. Fall in something other than love. Learn that you should've been seeing a chiropractor for years. Drink olive oil straight from the bottle.

676 square foot one-bedroom billed as a "rent-to-own" property, though several loopholes in the lease help the landlord

easily void this agreement. Live in the walk-in closet, go through old boxes, and read your pretentious notebook. Eat out. Get a dog. Think about engagement rings. Go to the gym. Self-publish a novel. Reconnect with Mom after Dad dies.

724 square foot one-bedroom. Live in this apartment until you die or get priced-out. Order in. Take up fishing but suck at it. Think about having kids. Paint the walls bright orange. Reread the classics and realize that you hate the classics. Buy eggs at the farmers market and throw them at a passing train. Tape off exactly 328 square feet and buy a futon.

Brother and Not-Brother

A few weeks after my brother's funeral, I saw him walking down Weidler. I made a beeline, arms outstretched. I exclaimed, "Paul? Is that you? You sonofabitch! You had me so worried. Really thought you were dead." Paul shuffled backward, and I laughed. This was his greatest con yet. I should've been angry, but the entire thing seemed funny.

Paul reached into his herringbone purse and fished around. "Stay back!" he commanded. His voice was too high-pitched and crisp, not strained from years of cigarettes.

"What the hell are you wearing? You scamming someone? Need money? I can help if you've got debts again," I said. He had talked about faking his death more than once. He was the kind of guy who always owed somebody something. But he was also generous. His friends always owed him too, so it usually balanced out.

Paul pulled something from his purse and spritzed my eyes. Viscous tears clouded everything. Shades of black, punctuated with reddish hues. Heeled shoes click-clacked away. Sure, we were no longer very close, but I didn't think things were that bad. I stumbled back to my apartment, smiling against the pain. I rinsed my eyes under the bathroom faucet. Through my blurred vision, I thought I saw Paul's silhouette. But it was just my reflection in the mirror.

The next few encounters were much like the first. Each time a new version of my brother brushed past, I assumed

I'd busted some elaborate ruse. I ran up to these lookalikes. I shook them and shouted, "Paul? Is that you?"

In response, each doppelganger would sneer and squirm loose. "Christ! I'm not Paul. Who's Paul? Who are you?" The voices were still off. Their clothes, too—pleather pants and wool skirts and fancy blazers and flannel shirts.

Everything else was spot-on. The eyes. The nose. The forearms, covered in my brother's tattoos. Stubby ears. High eyebrows. These copies of my brother even bit their nails. They all wore his usual dopey smile. He was such a happy guy, even when things went to shit. I wanted to hug all of them—but they wanted to get the fuck away from me.

I had just watched the guy go into the ground. I was a pallbearer, for fuck's sake! I'd seen his face, shellacked in the undertaker's makeup, an attempt to hide burst, hyperthermic blood vessels. Intellectually, I knew he was dead, but it was so hard to see him *everywhere* and not say hello, smile, laugh, cry. I wanted to spend time in those moments and reminisce about the distant years spent growing up together.

I soon discovered an outlet for this pent-up nostalgia. At work, the brother lookalikes had no choice but to interact. For eight hours of forced proximity, I could pretend he was still alive. I went to the marketing cubes and told Nicole every joke I knew from Laffy Taffy wrappers and Saturday morning cartoons. She beamed and laughed, and I basked in my brother's smile, over and over. I finally ruined it when I said, "Oh shit, like that time we burned that old canoe. Remember? We jettisoned it right onto the lake, and we—"

"What the hell are you talking about?" Nicole-brother asked.

"Never mind," I said, and I searched for another person to play pretend with. As long as these reminders were popping up, I figured I might as well enjoy myself. I didn't spend enough time with Paul when he was alive. As kids, sure, but not as an adult. I had my life in Portland, and he was in-and-out of rehab back home. It was easy to save it all for the obligatory holiday gatherings, where our collective familial longings spilled out over a couple beers.

"What are you doing in marketing? Go clean the breakroom," my boss—who also looked exactly like my brother—shouted from across the cubes. It was hard to take boss-brother seriously. I had flashbacks to afterparty cleanups, desperate to erase the evidence before Mom and Dad got home. "Come on! Get the lead out," boss-brother repeated.

"Like the lead in your ankle?" I prodded, remembering the time Paul accidentally shot his ankle with a BB gun. The ball remained in his ankle ever since, lodged against bone and cartilage, a bumpy testament to teenage mistakes. It felt so natural, a call-and-response to my brother's presence.

"Forget the breakroom. Let's have a talk in my office." Boss-brother crossed his brotherly arms, flexing the raunchiest of his pinup tattoos. I beamed and fought the urge to hug him. He closed the door behind us and placed a box of tissues on his desk. "You had a death in the family recently, right?"

"Yes," I said.

"Why are you so—" boss-brother began. He didn't finish, his face contorting into a scowl. I knew what he wanted to say: *Why are you so manic all the time? What the fuck is wrong with you?*

"I'm okay," I said.

"Whatever is going on with you, it's impacting your work. Take some mental health time."

I wanted to stay at work. The outside world was full of people who wouldn't play along. Boss-brother leaned back and drummed his well-bitten nails on his desk. "I'm serious. Sort this out by Monday, otherwise we'll need to talk about disciplinary action."

I called Sue from the train. "Yeah, off early," I said. "I'm on the Red Line right now. Should be back in the neighborhood soon. Wanna grab an early dinner and see a movie?"

"Sure."

She sounded like herself. But so did the others. "Just promise me you're not Paul," I said.

"What? I'm not—"

"I mean, put on lots of makeup. Okay? Wear that nice dress. How often do I get a day off? We're gonna paint the town," I proclaimed.

"It's a movie on a Thursday. Are we painting the town beige?"

"But won't it be fun to pretend like it's a fancy night out? Seriously. Nice dress. Super gaudy makeup, with that bright red lipstick you love," I said. I hoped these accoutrements would hide any parts of her that might've morphed into Paul. "I'll wear that new shirt you got me, too. It'll be fun."

"Fine, but dinner better be at someplace nice. I don't wanna feel overdressed."

"Deal," I said. "I'll meet you at your apartment in like—I don't know—maybe thirty minutes?"

Of course, when Sue opened her apartment door, the dress, lipstick, and sparkly necklace didn't help. Even with all the trappings of my girlfriend, she looked like my brother. It reminded me of the time he visited, and we went to Rocky Horror at the Clinton Street Theater, both of us in drag. Paul's dress was ill-fitting, but he walked in heels better than me.

I presented Sue-brother a bouquet of fresh cut roses—or as fresh as the corner bodega allows—and she leaned in for a kiss. I moved to the side and embraced her tight. She smelled like Paul too. Smoke with a hint of pine, like a campfire or a burning canoe.

"I missed you," I whispered. I hadn't admitted that to myself at the funeral. Before his death, those holiday visits had always felt like enough. And I had almost dreaded the thought of reconnecting more often. It felt like we were two people who shared blood but were wholly incompatible as friends. He had different interests, different friends now. The kind of friends that I outgrew.

"I just saw you last weekend," Sue-brother said.

"I know," I held her tighter. "I love you. I don't think I ever told you that."

"You said that last weekend too. Are you sure you want to go out? Let's just order pizza and rent a movie. You're kind of *off* today."

"Nah, I feel great." I smiled and kept embracing her.

"Nobody who feels great says it like that."

"Like what?"

"I don't know. It's your tone. It's all airy. Are you on morphine again?"

"No," I said, pulling back. I recalled the time Paul was doped up in the hospital. He had tied a rope to a friend's bumper and tried to glide behind the car on a skateboard. It didn't end well. In his post-injury, morphine-addled state, he kept telling the same joke and cackling. It was long and convoluted, and I only remembered the end. "I'm a potato," he said, beaming as if he had just conquered the world with that nonsensical punchline.

I mumbled "potato" to myself, and Sue-brother must've heard.

"You're definitely weird today. I'm ordering in."

"What about the nice dinner?" I asked, afraid that *ordering in* might mean she wanted to snuggle later too. I couldn't have sex with her—not like this. "I already called ahead and made reservations."

"Okay, fine," Sue-brother said.

At the restaurant, she ordered a sparkling cocktail. I thought of New Year's Eve senior year, when I sat on the roof with Paul, and we polished off several bottles of cheap sparkling wine together. We both confessed to having crushes on the same girl at school. We lit fireworks, and Paul held one of them a little too long, turning his left thumb into a nerve-damaged stump. "I wonder if we can get the waiter to light this candle," Sue-brother said. She picked up the little tealight.

"No, don't!" I shouted, fearful that the candle might burst in a second thumb-destroying blunder. Paul had such a poor track record with flame—the firework, the burning canoe, the grill, the chimney incident.

"This is what I meant earlier. Something's up. Talk to me," she demanded.

"I just need to get my head straight," I said. Sue-brother didn't look amused, her mouth collapsed into a tight snarl, pudgy brotherly nose pushed inward and wrinkling. She stayed like that a while, glaring. She wasn't going to let this go. There was no way I'd play it cool the rest of the night, so I tried to explain: "Okay, it's my brother. Everything reminds me of him."

"That's normal," Sue-brother said. "Back when Tiffany died, the littlest things would trigger a memory. It might not seem like it now, but eventually you can remember and be happy for the time you had." She reached out for my hand, and she leaned in for a kiss again, my brother's mouth pursed tight, Rocky Horror lipstick glistening. I pulled back and slid out of my chair.

"No, you don't understand. You—" I started but caught myself before saying, *You look like my brother.* I had enough common sense to know that such a confession would doom our relationship. I shook my head as if to suggest I had no words left to offer. Awkwardly bailing on our dinner plans felt safer than divulging any more details. I sighed and left Sue-brother alone in her fancy dress with her expensive cocktail and free breadbasket. She didn't say anything as I pushed past a crowd of diner-brothers and caught the next bus back to my apartment.

I kept my head down, avoiding eye contact with the bus-driver-brother and a cohort of passenger-brothers, each vying for the one seat without gum on it. I needed to get back indoors, where I could be alone and decompress, away from all these reminders of Paul. Away from this horde of laughing, smiling, boisterously alive brothers.

I turned on my Xbox, certain I could lose myself in some zombie-blasting goodness, but even the game avatars became Paul. I rummaged through my junk drawer looking for something to occupy my time. Crossword puzzle to the rescue.

3-across: your brother (four letters)
4-down: also your brother (four letters)
7-down: your brother again (four letters)

I pulled a novel off my bookshelf and found every character was now simply *Paul*. It made for rather confusing and anticlimactic reading. In chapter three, Paul told Paul that Paul was divorcing Paul because Paul had slept with Paul. "Shit!" I shouted to an empty room.

I opened the fire escape window for some air, breathing deep and closing my eyes. The squeak of my brother's sneakers echoed below. The honk of his car horn blared. My phone vibrated, and the caller ID said *Paul*. I answered, and it was Sue cursing me out. I said, "I'm sorry. I'll make it right. I'll figure this out."

"You better," she said, and in that moment, her inflection changed. Her voice dropped an octave and took on a slight smoker's wheeze. "I know you're going through a lot right now, and—" my brother's voice continued. I hung up and turned off my phone.

There was no running from this. Everyone was Paul. I could either resist or join the group. Maybe it wouldn't feel so strange. Maybe it'd be like I was back home in Wisconsin, back with the family, whole again.

I broke open some Bic pens, got a safety pin, and began recreating Paul's tattoos. When I ran out of ink, I wiped away the blood and used a Sharpie to draw the rest. Next, I shattered a highball glass and pushed a small piece of glass into my ankle, desperate to recreate a facsimile of my brother's BB gun wound. I held my thumb to the flame on the stove until it blackened and blistered like Paul's Black Cat accident. I wanted to relive our greatest moments with all their pain and vibrancy. I wanted to remember what it was like to be young and have the world ahead of us. I wanted to feel like my body was as invincible and permanent as Paul's. I wanted to be happy, like he always was.

I inspected my bloodied handiwork in the bathroom mirror, but it wasn't enough. A battered version of myself stared back. I told myself the jokeless punchline: "I'm a potato." My smile found a shape somewhere between Paul's big grin and my usual close-lipped smirk.

Migratory Patterns

On the day I met Alexi, a gazillion birds descended on Couch Park. They perched on trees, benches, and playground equipment, and they spread across the grass. The mass of birds became so dense that some smaller birds had to stand atop larger birds. But this wasn't some Hitchcock thing. Sure, a couple people freaked out, but mostly it was peaceful, beautiful. There were bird varietals I'd never seen before, not even at the zoo (then again, the Portland Zoo doesn't have many birds to begin with). The entire color wheel was represented with feathers and beaks and stick-thin legs. They'd fly away in shifts to forage, always returning to the gigantic bird cluster to share the spoils.

    I discovered Alexi at a coffee shop nearby. That one with the chess tables set up near the front. It wasn't a usual haunt, but it was close to the park, and I didn't want to wander too far from the birds. I ordered my usual drip coffee (quick and simple), and, in my hurry, I bumped into this cute guy. He spilled cappuccino all over himself. I offered to buy him a new drink, but then he complained about the dry cleaning bill. "Just text me with the total, and I'll take care of it," I said. I handed him my number, glad that the circumstances provided a built-in excuse for me to pass out my digits.

    He glanced at the number, up at me, at the number again, and then he smiled. It was like he didn't realize that I was also cute until the cappuccino had time to cool (yeah, it's conceited, but I know I'm cute—sometimes I'd prefer to be hot, which is way different, but I'll take cute). I should've been insulted that he didn't 'notice' me right away, but I was too busy admiring his adorable glasses and weird little haircut. It looked like he took great effort with the hairdo, but it was designed in a way to belie such efforts, faux bedhead that takes hours to perfect (what do they call that, shabby chic?—no, that's a term for distressed furniture—is it grungy?).

I went back to watch the birds while checking my phone every ten minutes. Of course, I told myself he wouldn't text until the next day (or two). Play it cool. But I knew he'd text eventually, and not just about the dry cleaning bill. Some of the birds began chirping in pseudo-unison (actual unison is hard when you're dealing with a gazillion of anything—plenty of well-intentioned birds messed up the timing). I felt like they were singing for me, and by nightfall I was sure of it. People brought out lawn chairs and set them up along the sidewalk. When the sidewalk filled, more lawn chairs spilled out onto Glisan. Police officers showed up. They were decked out in riot gear. I think they had been deployed to clear the blocked street. But when they saw the birds, they understood, and they redirected traffic away from Glisan.

I stayed until morning, lounging on the grass at that Jewish temple across the street. I fell asleep for a couple hours before my phone vibrated. We had our first date at Bartini. I was sleep deprived, so the entire first date was foggy, but I remembered a vague sense of enjoying myself. He talked a lot about his work (architectural something—not architectural design, but close—maybe it was architectural development?—is that a thing?). He subtly alluded to a 401k and other things that suggested a budget and a better life-plan than mine. I told him about my graduate program and how one of the creepy professors was constantly hitting on students. Talk turned to music and hiking, then it devolved into non-specific over-enthusiasm with each additional cocktail. All in all, no bombshells to report, and some inklings of a good time worth chasing. I slammed a Red Bull and went to work. I was groggy but happy. It had been a good twenty-four hours.

We decided to meet at Couch Park and watch the birds for our second date. Traffic was completely screwed up in the immediate area. We strolled through standstill cars and buses as we neared the park. Glisan was still packed full, and Nineteenth and Hoyt were crowded too. The temple had a bunch of tents set up on the grounds, and some rabbi guy was going around pulling out stakes, feebly shooing the trespassers away. Normally, the temple people don't care (I've had lengthy picnics on their lawn before), but can you blame them for dissuading a shantytown?

There was nowhere to sit, so we stood until our legs went numb. The birds sang again, and they took turns swooping through the sky in tightly organized clusters. I eventually realized that there wasn't any birdshit on the ground. In addition to feeding in groups, they must've been toileting off-site. I think the birds knew they were beautiful (way better than cute or hot), and they didn't want to ruin the aesthetic of their massive, colorful display.

We smoked a joint and kissed twice. It was a good second date. I would've asked him over to my place, but I was too tired for anything but sleep, and I got the impression that he liked to move slow. No need to hurry. Things were going well, and there would be more dates soon. A bright yellow bird cluster took its turn skyward while the sun set. It was like the birds were doing their part to balance out the disappearing light. I swear their feathers were glowing, just a little.

On our third date, we watched the birds for a couple hours, then we got sushi at San Sai. We talked about movies (mostly documentaries) and books (mostly mystery novels) and wine (mostly cheap twist-offs). We ordered saké for dessert, and I soon discovered that we weren't actually taking it slow. We went back to his place: a swanky open concept apartment in the Pearl District. We made love until the gigantic apartment smelled of cum and sweat. Then we donned bathrobes and went onto his balcony (yeah, he had a balcony). We smoked together. He watched the unmoving cityscape as if the buildings might shift at any moment. He said he was trying to see the bridges in the distance. He started to tell me how Portland's bridges were a feat of engineering and design and how he studied them in grad school. I'd already heard about the bridges a gazillion times from a gazillion Portlanders, but I pretended to listen.

While he pointed into the darkness, pretending like he could see the bridge, a pink and blue bird landed on a nearby ledge. It was all alone. It was the first of the birds I had seen solo. They seemed to move in packs (or flocks, I suppose). It had a big goiter-like beak, sort of like a pelican. The bird sneezed (I didn't know birds could sneeze). It hopped around a bit. It nibbled at nothing in particular on the ledge. Then it wobbled and fell off the ledge. When it hit the concrete, it sounded like the time my upstairs neighbor had a heart attack (a loud thud as she hit the hardwood floor, reverberating throughout the building). I screamed, or shrieked, or made some other terrible sound, and Alexi held me. "What is it?" he asked.

"You didn't see that?"

"See what?"

I pointed to the grotesque, broken creature, its wing bent backward and one stick-thin leg completely broken off. He said it was too dark. He couldn't see the bird, just like I couldn't see the bridges.

The next morning, he made me eggs. It was a sweet gesture (although, it was a bit cliché—I mean, come on, eggs?—he could've made something more exotic—maybe something that took more than two minutes to cook—a mimosa or Bloody Mary would've been nice too). I thanked him for the eggs but said I couldn't eat anything related to birds. He laughed, but I didn't think it was funny. He apologized and made me some microwavable French toast sticks. I think the sticks contained powdered eggs, but I ate them anyway.

On my way to work, I passed Couch Park. The crowd had thinned a little. The shantytown only covered half the temple grounds, whereas it had previously annexed every square foot. The rabbi had his own chair set up next to one of the squatters. They were having a beer together. I thought rabbis couldn't drink, but I'm not Jewish, so that might not be true.

When I got to work, a fluffy bird with green and orange stripes was dead on the stoop. I got some tongs from the back room and placed the bird in a shoebox. I decided I'd give it a proper burial.

After work, I went to Alexi's neighborhood, searching the sidewalk for the pink and blue bird. I felt guilty for leaving it and thought it needed a burial too. I couldn't find it anywhere. Some custodian or groundskeeper for Alexi's building probably took it away, maintaining the high-end building's glamour compared to the newspaper tumbleweeds and discarded cigarettes of lesser apartment complexes.

Alexi spotted me and shouted something from his balcony. I couldn't hear him, so I dialed his number. "What are you doing here?" he asked, sounding somewhat annoyed.

"Looking for the dead bird?"

"Why?"

"To give it a proper burial?"

"Why?"

"Because it's the right thing to do."

"If you wanted to come over, you could've asked," he said.

Maybe this was his version of coyness or flirtation, but I wasn't in the mood. "If you want to help me you can, but I'm not here to chat," I said.

He got dressed and came down. We tried to go to Couch Park for the burial, but the birds wouldn't budge. There wasn't a single fleck of birdless ground for us to walk on. We tried to push through, and they pecked at our shins. We gave up after a large Froot Loops-type bird drew blood. In that moment, it felt a little more like Hitchcock, but still not really. The birds didn't follow us as we left. They weren't aggressive, just defensive.

We buried the fluffy green and orange bird in a shallow grave in Forest Park. I think Alexi rolled his eyes at one point. Since I wasn't sure, I didn't get pissed or call him on it. Even if he was annoyed, I was still grateful that he indulged my inexplicable mourning (I knew the whole thing seemed pretentious anyway—the bird funeral could've been ripped from the script of some hip new indie film destined to sweep Cannes).

We got dinner at the theater pub that night. We left before the movie even started (the film probably wouldn't have achieved bird funeral grandeur anyway). We went back to my place. He said he liked my wall art. I told him that I hated it, but I had felt like the walls needed something, so I grabbed all the tacky art the thrift store had to offer. With that, he decided he hated it too. I told him about my dissertation research (a qualitative study of PTSD onset among incarcerated veterans), and he paid moderate attention. Penelope meowed in the corner and batted around a toy.

We talked about movies. I couldn't remember which documentaries we both liked because the ones that came up in conversation seemed like polar opposites. We had sex until my studio apartment smelled like cum and shit. We got dressed and went downstairs to smoke. "I'd better get home," he said. I thought I'd be sad, but I really didn't care that he wasn't spending the night.

When I went back upstairs, Penelope was still playing with her toy. "Bring it here," I said (Penelope likes to play fetch, which I guess is unusual for a cat). She dropped a dead bird at my feet. It looked like a common finch. It probably didn't come from the Couch Park spectacle; the finch wasn't ornate enough to be part of the show. I almost forgot other birds existed. I didn't bother burying it. I threw it in the dumpster downstairs. I smoked another joint, ate some Cheetos, and went to bed alone.

The following day, the crowd demographics changed a bit. There were more campers and expensive pop-up lawn chairs (the ones with cup holders built-in). I think it was the out-of-state crowd finally arriving to witness the birds. There were vendors selling bird popsicles (regular popsicles with crappy beaks and wings molded onto them), and T-shirts, and a bunch of kitschy feathered stuff.

The birds sang in near-unison, ruffled their feathers, and put on a good show, but it didn't seem as impressive as before. How often could you just sit and look at a bunch of birds? And what if I wanted to read a book in Couch Park? It was practically ceded to the birds. The mayor even gave some speech, rechristening the park "Avian Park" (such a generic name with no pizzazz).

I went to work and texted Alexi. We arranged to meet for drinks at some dive bar off of Burnside. We made out in the bathroom for a minute before I said, "This is trashy, let's go back to your place." We fucked twice, and the apartment stank of cum and blood. I told him I wanted to go home.

On the way back, I passed the park. The shantytown had dwindled a little. I think the newcomers had retired to hotel rooms for the night. Glisan was still blocked with a few people sleeping in their lawn chairs, but Hoyt and Nineteenth had both cleared. Some of the birds squawked a little, but most slept. I ducked into another bar and got a vodka tonic. I went home, crawled in bed, and gave Penelope a new toy (a plush mouse on a string), but she didn't seem interested.

The following night, Alexi wanted me to come over again. I texted back, *No, but we should talk*. We went to a tea house. I had some Earl Grey, and he had a water. He said, "I hate tea."

I said, "This isn't working out."

"What? Because I don't like tea?"

"No, that's not it. I thought we clicked. But now I don't know. I just don't think I'm looking for a relationship," I said (that was a lie—I was looking for a relationship, but I could tell that what Alexi and I had wasn't turning into one).

"Oh, you're one of those people."

"Whatever, I'm not here to fight. I just wanted to be mature about this. Maybe we can get coffee sometime, but that's it."

He mumbled something. He might've said, "Fuck you." I'm not sure. After he finished grumbling, we had a semi-cordial chat about artwork (he liked cubism—I liked impressionism). I felt like it was our first authentic conversation ever (it was also our last—we never got coffee 'sometime'—I heard he got married, proposed to somebody on the Hawthorne Bridge).

On the way home, I passed three dead birds. Blue, green, and some gigantic purple one. I decided to walk through the park again. As I approached, I didn't hear anything. And in that instant, I felt that all the birds would be gone. I imagined Couch Park reverted to the way it was and always had been, before Alexi and before the birds. The birds had arrived when we met, and it seemed fitting that they'd vanish as quickly. Perhaps a few carcasses, or piles of feathers, maybe an egg or two left behind.

But as I rounded Glisan, they were all still there. The gigantic horde actually seemed a bit more colorful and densely packed than before, like the most distant tropical flocks had finally arrived, joining the gathering en masse. The birds didn't care that we broke up (or stopped fucking each other—I guess you can't 'break up' if you've never officially been a couple). I bought a popsicle (or birdsicle, I suppose), and I pried a mostly-full beer from the sleeping rabbi's hand. I nursed the beer, watching the birds rise and fall in small groups, leaving and rejoining the collective.

The birds began singing again. I drank and listened to the arrhythmic tune until sunup. As I yawned and stretched in the summer sun, I felt like if I walked into the center of Couch Park, the birds might accept me as one of their own. I pretended that, if only for an instant, I was one of them.

Fruit Rot

Lacey and I need money. She's depressed again, and we can't afford therapy. I've been working nights at a convenience store, and she sells tchotchke crap on Etsy—which only makes matters worse, because she'd rather be crafting something worthwhile or working on a new painting. On a daily basis, she asks, "Why do shitty fridge magnets sell, but nobody buys anything *real* online?" Then she mumbles about how 3D printed bullshit is swallowing her Etsy store whole, and she skips dinner. She puts up a pissed-off front, but underneath she's just sad. I think that's sort of what Frank Castle is actually like, hiding behind that macho *Punisher* stuff. Lacey takes St. John's Wort from Walgreens. The bottle touts a natural remedy for "mood improvement." It doesn't work. She says she needs real drugs, but that takes real money.

I storyboard my new superhero comic. It's about a guy who discovers Old MacDonald's secret GMO lab, and then he mutates into a super strong half-pig hybrid thing and uses his power to fight for food justice. I'm going for some kind of subtle satire, but Lacey says it's not subtle at all. Her exact words are, "That's so fucking obvious. And Old MacDonald? Like from the nursery rhyme? Really?"

I prepare a pitch anyway. The rep for Dynamite tells me, "Nobody wants *new* heroes. Too much Marvel and DC oversaturation. If you ain't working with an existing IP and a built-in fan base, then forget it. Superheroes are played out.

Write something real or try Dark Horse." The Dark Horse guy just says "No" without much explanation. The rep for Image won't even meet with me.

I try to write something real. I write about Lacey and how she was beaten by her father. But by page three she already discovers that she's part of a secret society that protects humanity from aliens. Her dad becomes an alien on page ten, and she kills him on page twelve. I toss the draft after page sixteen, wherein Lacey's newly upgraded robotic arm malfunctions. What the fuck is wrong with me?

I show the storyboards to Lacey, and she says, "Of course it sucks. You don't even know the whole story with my dad. And it's not like you can write vicariously through my past traumas."

"But what about the alien part? That was kind of cool, right?"

She doesn't respond, but her look is answer enough.

I need some fresh air and a fresh perspective. I limp out of the bedroom, shuffle around the hole in our stairs, and sit on the porch. I prop my messed-up leg on the nearby footstool and lean back. I want to do some pensive skyline staring, like in the movies, but there's a tree blocking my view. There wasn't a tree yesterday. Not even a bud. Our front yard has always been a barren dirt patch.

This mystery tree is huge, and the bark is a perfect Silver Age green, like it jumped right off the *Incredible Hulk #2* cover. The tree has sparkly leaves and golden fruit sprouting from its nuclear green arms. The fruit is round like an orange, but shiny like a ripe apple.

"Lacey, there's a tree in our yard," I say.

"No there isn't," Lacey yells from inside.

"Yes there is," I say. I pluck a golden fruit from the tree as proof. I drop it on Lacey's desk.

She looks up from her hot glue gun. "Oh, I see," she says.

"Can we eat it?" I ask.

"That's your first thought? Eating it?"

"It could help reduce our food bills," I say. "Maybe we can use the savings to patch the hole in the stairs."

"The savings? I don't think our annual fruit budget is all that big," she says.

I take a bite. It tastes like Pixy Stix.

I offer Lacey a taste, but before she bites it, the fruit turns blackish, and small bugs crawl from its dark flesh. Lacey shrieks and throws the fruit. It splats against the floor, oozing black guts and sending a cadre of bugs scurrying into the floorboards. "What the hell! It's rotten," she screams.

"It tasted fine to me. I'll get something to clean it up," I say. I take a step toward the kitchen, and my knee doesn't buckle. I take a second step; the joint is smooth. I grab a dish towel and sprint back across the house. My messed-up leg feels brand new. In fact, my entire body seems fine-tuned. There are none of the usual aches and throbs that accompany the movements of a middle-aged man with no health insurance, no exercise regimen, and a food stamp diet.

Lacey and I pluck some more fruit that evening and try to bake a pie. Within a few seconds of slicing into the fruit, its flesh turns black and spews bugs again. I spend the rest of the night hunting and smashing bugs with my shoe. I'm secretly glad for the opportunity to chase the insects; it lets me show off my newly rediscovered fine-motor skills, sharp reflexes, and limp-free leg. I can't decide if I feel like Superman after he soaks up rejuvenating sunbeams or Batman when he gets that kickass supersuit in Frank Miller's magnum opus. Probably Superman, since Batman was getting mechanical assistance—but in truth, I'd rather be Batman.

I begin redrafting my Old MacDonald character. He turns into Ronald McDonald. I try to make him more devious and scary, and he becomes something like a hillbilly farmer crossed with the Joker. The concept sketch doesn't make any sense, but I like the weird image of Joker with a pitchfork, so I put it on the fridge using one of Lacey's Etsy magnets.

Next week, Lacey gets the flu. On a hunch, I ask her to eat the fruit.

"What if it gets gross again?" she asks.

"It seems okay," I tell her. "I think it only gets rotten after it's cut open."

She gives me a strange glance while taking a quick bite and a slow swallow. The remaining portion of fruit turns black and buggy in her hand. I hold up a small trashcan, but Lacey misses the can, and the black goop slides down the wall.

"How do you feel?" I ask.

"Good," she says. She sounds hesitant, like she doesn't believe the transformation. She takes her temperature. It's normal. She takes it again. Normal. Again. Normal. She goes to the bathroom mirror and inspects her nasal passages. She tries to blow her nose and nothing comes out. She takes her temperature again. I leave her to her inspections.

After an hour, she comes downstairs. "Babe, I'm one hundred percent better," she says with more confidence.

"I know," I say.

"No, listen to me. One hundred percent. Not just the flu. My hysterectomy scars are gone. That kink in my neck is gone. Everything. I feel new."

I drain my pitiful bank account and put an ad in the paper. Lacey says, "Nobody reads the paper," and she puts an ad on Craigslist instead. Twelve people show up for our miracle fruit. Eleven respond from Craigslist—they are sick and need cures. One responds from the newspaper ad—he's a lawyer from some ambulance-chaser firm specializing in frivolous lawsuits. The lawyer hands us some watermarked forms about a violation for bringing an invasive species into the neighborhood, something about FDA noncompliance, and a lawsuit for false advertising. He puts away the eco-violation after a woman's goiter shrinks. He pockets the FDA paperwork when an ex-boxer's cauliflower ear reforms into its original shape. And he ditches the false advertising claim when a gaunt, cancer-ridden woman regains pigment, regrows hair, and rises from her wheelchair. By the time all eleven people are cured, the lawyer wants to buy a piece of fruit for some unseen ailment. Lacey tells him it'll be double. He grumbles and obliges.

The next day, word of mouth delivers us dozens of new clients. Lacey tries to explain supply and demand to me while painting over yesterday's prices with much, much higher rates. A few years ago, Lacey took some business courses, back when she had dreams of opening her own gallery. She knows what she's doing, and I'm pleased to see her smile again as she uses words like "market value" and "scarcity principle." The way she's talking, with such enthusiasm, it reminds me of when she was in grad school, pontificating about Frida Kahlo at length over a mug of red wine.

We sell even more fruit than the day before, despite the higher prices. I decide it's best to let Lacey handle all business-related fruit issues. She knows what she's doing. She hires the ambulance-chaser lawyer that we met on our first day of sales. He's the only lawyer we know, but he insists he's good at his job. Together, they form an LLC, get our house rezoned for agricultural production and sale, and schedule local TV and radio spots for promotion of this groundbreaking startup venture. Meanwhile, I use some of the profits to fix the hole in our stairs—now that my leg is healed, I don't want it getting fucked up again.

When Lacey announces the grand reopening for our newly zoned yard, a line stretches past the horizon. Our fruit tree attracts sickly people, movie stars, news crews, research scientists who want to synthesize this miracle cure, and self-proclaimed millionaires who say money is no object. Lacey raises the price several more times. She teaches me how to use spreadsheets, and we track the progress of our exponential bank account. In less than a month, we go from Peter Parker dirt-shit poor to Bruce Wayne mega wealthy.

But we soon face a different problem: the huge demand, falling supply, and sky-high prices breed desperate sob stories. People take off their clothes and show us their sickly bodies in hopes of pity. Mothers and fathers tell us about dying children. Pity. Guilt. Sorrow. We want to help everybody, but we don't want to deplete all the fruit. I can already see barren patches where we've plucked too many—I don't notice any new blossoms or buds, so I'm not sure if this tree will keep producing. I track it all on my fancy spreadsheets. I show Lacey the numbers, she applauds my newfound business acumen, and we both decide that we need to carefully manage our remaining supply.

We hire a contractor to erect fences around our property to protect ourselves from the mob. We interview security guards, and the lawyer helps us with background checks and tax paperwork for our new employees. With these measures, it feels like a cross between a regular business and a prison, complete with razor wire and floodlights.

The perimeter now secure, we chart a more reasonable plan for daily sales. I take inventory of the remaining fruit globes. I prepare a brief report for Lacey—she is, after all, the CFO, CEO, and President of our LLC. Basically, the report recommends that we only sell one fruit per day. At that rate, the supply will last us for a couple months. With estimated golden fruit market growth rates, those couple months will net enough income for us to live comfortably for our entire lives.

We post a sign saying *One Customer Per Day*, and the crowd screams. The guards form a barrier, brandish clubs, and order is restored. Some people cry, and I need to look away. I remind myself that the money from our sales will help Lacey and me. She'll no longer burn herself with a glue gun and use it as an excuse to let out a week's worth of sobs. And maybe after the right medication and some more therapy sessions, she'll know what's making her sad, and we can work on it together. Then we can get married, and maybe we'll get a cat named Selina—after Catwoman, of course.

We make a single sale to somebody claiming to work for Apple. He says the fruit can bring Steve Jobs back to life, but I don't think the fruit works that way. He signs the waiver, and the lawyer gives his seal of approval, so it's no longer my problem. After the two-minute transaction, we close shop and the guards shoot beanbags at the crowd in controlled bursts followed by a teargas finale.

I lock the gate and spend time on a new comic. I sit underneath the fruit tree, and I write stories about similarly strange trees with mysterious origins, and this gives way to a character who can control trees. And soon enough there are vines and flowers and a whole family of plants. The character loves the plants and treats them like his own children. In turn, they love him, and they obey his commands. At first I think it's artsy and that I'm doing a magical realist story rather than a superhero motif. But when I show five splash pages to Lacey, she says, "So it's a superhero with plant powers or something? I guess that's kinda cool. A little different from having animal powers."

"No, it's not a superhero story," I say.

"Yeah, it is."

I look at the sketch again. I realize she's right. I've created a good-guy version of something like Poison Ivy. I think my character is dissimilar enough that I won't get sued by DC, but I ask the lawyer anyway. He says it's not his area of legal expertise, but he thinks I'm safe. I draw some more vines and globes of golden fruit dangling underneath the character's arms, and I decide that I like the concept. I want to work on this project. It feels right. So what if superheroes are played out? Lacey and I pull a huge fruit-seller salary now, and I can afford to self-publish. I can do it right. A brand new IP with heroics, melodrama, and out-of-this-world stories. All I need is a villain. You can't have Batman without Joker. Spiderman needs Doctor Octopus. Superman needs Lex Luthor.

At first I use the sketch of Lacey's dad again—in extraterrestrial form, of course. I think that maybe the aliens want to invade, but they breathe carbon dioxide, so they are killing off the earth's plants to deplete the atmospheric oxygen, sort of like terraforming. And they're secretly responsible for promoting fossil fuel consumption and stifling the green revolution. And maybe the plant-hero-guy protects the forest and fights these aliens. It sounds stupider the more I outline the plot. It'll never do.

I draw another sketch of farmer Joker trying to inject pesticides into the superhero's plant children. Lacey walks by and laughs. It isn't supposed to be funny, but I'm glad she's laughing so much now. And I'm glad I'm brainstorming more each day. And I'm glad I don't wake from stress dreams about our finances.

The next day, the first person in line cannot afford our price. Neither can the second. Or the third. We hear sob story after sob story as we work through the window-shoppers. About two dozen people into the line, somebody finally ponies up the dough—a woman with a bandaged arm, a leg that bends the wrong way, and a burn on one half of her face. She reminds me of Two Face, and I think about knockoff versions that might work with my story—a plant that's dipped in acid, or maybe a greedy CEO who flips a coin to decide which rainforests to destroy.

The crowd tries to push through. The guards conk a few heads with their nightsticks, and that seems to be the end of it. The woman wipes off the fruit. "Just in case you use pesticides," she says.

"We don't," I say.

"Can't ever be too careful."

She takes a bite of the golden prize. Her arm makes popping noises as it reassembles itself beneath the bandages. Her leg and foot do a one-eighty, and her red face becomes soft and flesh-toned again. Most of the crowd and the guards are awestruck at the instant healing process—they've seen others eat the fruit, but most illnesses are less visible.

Taking advantage of the distraction, a scrawny guy with lesions all over his body bolts through the crowd and grabs the woman's fruit. The guards swing their batons, but they can't connect with the agile man. He does a tuck-and-roll maneuver, skidding to a stop near the base of the tree. He holds up the stolen, half-eaten fruit. It blackens and bugs coat his hands. He closes his eyes and bites it anyway. Nothing happens. "What the fuck?" he says, as rotten, tar-like juice drips from his mouth. The guards smack his kneecaps, and he goes down. The guards pummel him; he loses a tooth and his fingers bend backwards.

A reporter is lingering nearby, wrapping up a puff piece on the hopefuls and marveling at the woman's arm. The reporter interviews the fruit thief immediately after the guards redeposit him amongst the ever-growing crowd.

The lawyer releases a statement: "He was trespassing on private property, he stole company property, and the company had every right to forcibly recover aforementioned property." The news team documents his injuries. We get phone calls from other networks within five minutes. A helicopter is overhead in ten. I release another statement, offering to pay his medical bills in a show of good faith. I don't even notice the funds leaving our bank account—these thousands of dollars are meaningless now. The goodwill gesture pacifies people momentarily, until a camera crew visits the guy's home. The crew discovers his family turned to blackish, shriveled corpses. They visit the scrawny guy in the hospital. There's a close-up on the scrawny guy's agony as he watches the footage of his dead family.

The lawyer recommends we do some testing. Without accurate data, he can't assess our liability. I know I should be more horrified, more empathetic, more anything other than defensive—but somehow, all I can think to do is protect the business. The business *does* help people, after all. Our once-daily customer is cured. It's a miracle. Lacey and I provide miracles. And we're finally living our own lives. We're happy. I didn't used to be happy. And there's something about being happy that makes you want to keep being happy. And it's hard to keep being happy if you're thinking about the shittiness of everybody else's lives.

We hire a scientist for a ridiculous sum of money—this time, I notice the difference at the ATM. The scientist purchases lab mice that all come from distinct breeding lines. She keeps each biological family unit in different cages and tests her hypothesis. She feeds a mouse some rotten fruit. It has no effect on the mouse who ingests it, but the entire immediate family shrivels and dies in a rush of black blood and grotesque mousy shrieks and chirps. She repeats the test a dozen times and introduces control groups of unrelated mice. The results are always the same: ingesting rotten fruit kills off the entire immediate family.

I sit in front of the few mice still alive in the lab. I write about a new villain and attempt a sketch. She's an evil scientist who breeds super mice that infect people with some mystery illness. The infected people have black blood, and they commit atrocious murders. Eventually, almost every human on earth falls ill, and the plant-hero-guy worries it'll spread to trees next. So he develops a robot army to fight the murderous, infected masses. The robots rip open the diseased corpses and drink the black blood for fuel, and I realize I've drawn General Blackblood from *2000AD*, so I backtrack.

In my next version, the diseased mice bite the scientist, and she turns into a rodent. My preliminary sketches look like Splinter from *TMNT*. Why the fuck is it so hard to come up with an original villain? Hell, I don't even care if it's original—it can be another rip-off—I just want it to feel natural. I want the hero/villain struggle to be embedded into every aspect of the story. I want the reader to know the stakes from page one, and I want to recapture that epic struggle of good versus evil. I need a grotesque, bad-to-the-bone Venom, not some complicated Harry Osborn shit.

None of it's working. I crumple the pages and relay the scientist's findings to Lacey and the lawyer.

"Shit," Lacey says. She pokes a dead mouse with a pencil.

"Yeah, I know. It sucks. I don't want this to happen again. We need more security," I say.

"No, you need more lawyers," the lawyer says.

We hire both. We also add high-tech cameras, motion sensors, knockout gas, and snares.

Even though the lawyer says we could've won the suit,

Lacey and I decide it's best to settle with the scrawny guy out of court. The lawyer and his new legal team update the waiver and assure us that our liability is zero again.

The line still stretches past the horizon, despite the bad press. Lacey is hesitant to open again, but we have to sell some fruit, otherwise we'll run dry—all the security and legal fees are pricey, and Lacey has appointments to see an expensive celebrity therapist twice a week now.

After the grand re-reopening, things go smoothly for about a week.

The next security breach is better planned than the scrawny guy's mad dash. As a wealthy man exits with his expensive fruit locked in an icebox, a woman slips past the gate before it clanks shut. She's got a gas mask, and she is unfazed by the chemical mist enveloping her small frame. Her Kevlar vest repels beanbag rounds. But all this heavy equipment doesn't help her outmaneuver the squad of guards. They tackle her. I warn them not to hurt her too badly—we don't want more negative press. She puts up a fight, but they eventually toss her outside.

We close shop and map out some new security measures. As the blueprints grow, we discover that we've outlined plans for a fortress, and even the once-daily customer will have a tough time getting in. I put down my pencil and suggest a different approach: "What if we stop letting anybody inside?"

"What do you mean?" Lacey asks.

"Look at the security we already have. It's crazy. But people are still getting through. Let's get rid of the line altogether. Get rid of the risk," I say.

"How will that work?"

"Maybe we can buy out the neighbors. I'm sure they're sick of how our whole block is a media circus now, and they'd gladly sell. We lock it down and give the guards permission to incapacitate anybody setting foot on the exterior properties. Have some peace and quiet again."

"I'm still not seeing it. I mean, we do have a chunk of change saved, but what about keeping the business going? We have more expenses now. And that woman from today might sue."

"If she does, we can win."

"Yeah, but we need money to win. And I want to buy that gallery downtown, and what about self-publishing your comic and hiring a publicist for it? We need to keep selling. You wanna go back to how it was before?"

"No, I'm not saying that. Let's set up a foundation. We can have the foundation read through all the requests for fruit and make some autonomous decisions. Take us out of the loop. Freeze the fruit and ship everything off-site with one of those armored trucks like banks use. Keep it on ice in a vault somewhere. No more of this daily stuff. Release a few pieces of fruit per year. Keep prices really high. Let the lawyers sort it out."

"I guess that could work," Lacey says. "So, basically, we'd be retiring?"

I shrug. "Sort of. We'd still collect checks."

We pluck most of the fruit, leaving a few dangling near the top of the tree—our private reserve. We vacuum pack the fruit, freeze it, and hand it off to the lawyers, a security team, and the foundation's newly appointed president. We watch our stress level fall and our bank account rise once more. We keep seeing more zeroes at the end of each statement, even as we make gigantic withdrawals to buy out and fortify the entire neighborhood.

Along with more security, we decide to make other improvements. We use a portion of our newfound wealth to convert the house next door into a full-service spa. We let the guards use it every now and then, but it's mostly for us. We gut an open-concept house and turn it into a basketball court—this is mainly so I can continue to show off my limp-free leg to nobody in particular. Lacey fashions the corner property into a future gallery space, deciding it's better than buying one downtown—neither of us want to be too far from the private fruit reserve or the comfortable amenities of our new, sprawling compound.

Next, we renovate our house. We get new appliances, hardwood floors, granite countertops, new insulation, new plumbing, new wiring. The works. The entire place looks shiny and perfect.

We designate the attic and basement for our personal whims. Lacey converts the attic into an artist's loft, and she celebrates by purchasing a huge canvas, super expensive zebra-hair paintbrushes, and seven crates of assorted paints. She burns her Etsy tchotchkes beneath the tree with its sparkling leaves and golden fruit, and she dances amid the shimmering reflections and roaring flames. In a display of unfettered joy, she leaps through the fire and burns her ankles—but she eats a piece of fruit and restores her legs to their original state. Meanwhile, I convert the basement into a Batcave replica. I buy an authentic Batsuit signed by Michael Keaton. I wire all our new surveillance equipment to LCD screens in the Batcave. It's like the real deal.

I spend most nights in the basement Batcave while Lacey paints for hours in the attic studio. We consistently meet back up at midnight to rediscover the sexual spark we had years ago.

For a while, I keep the Batsuit in a glass display case, not wanting to risk tainting its pristine condition. But eventually my impulse control breaks down, and I wear the thing around the Batcave. I draw some new villains, but they all turn into a variant of the Joker fused with some other Batman character. The Joker and Robin hybrid is by far the most amusing new sketch, but it doesn't get me closer to a usable villain—and it's still not as good as my original Joker farmer sketch.

I try to reboot my brainstorming session with a sketch of Lacey, but she turns out looking like Harley Quinn. I'm about to try again when the Batcave lights up. Warning LEDs flicker and three cameras go dark. I run outside. A woman sits atop the razor-wire wearing a thick burlap bodysuit designed to keep the wire from flaying her skin. She sprays black paint on a fourth camera. She hops to the ground and reminds me of a burlap-clad Catwoman. The guards pelt her with beanbags. She doesn't go down.

The woman bolts toward the fruit tree. Some snares encircling the tree snap to life, and she writhes on the ground. The guards zip tie her hands while I remove the snares. One guard shines a Maglite on her face. It's the same woman who first outwitted the knockout gas countermeasures. "Stay off our property," I say.

"I just want one," she says.

"So does everybody else. It wouldn't be fair to give you one while other people plead their case and wait their turn. Submit your request to the foundation," I say.

"No, you don't understand," she says.

"Yes, I do," I say, and I decide I've had enough. I gesture for the guards to take her away. I go back inside. I sit down, and the Batsuit's cape bunches beneath my ass. I wriggle around and shove the cape aside. It's only then that I realize I was dressed as a superhero while I told a pleading woman that I couldn't help her. I pull off the black mask and throw it into the glass display case. "Fuck!" I scream out loud. I never wanted any of this.

I decide that maybe I need therapy too. I go upstairs to ask Lacey about it—I've never been to therapy before, and it sounds kind of iffy. She holds up a pregnancy test strip with two lines on it. "I guess the fruit healed my uterus too."

"What? How? It was gone. Removed completely," I grab the test strip and shake it, thinking maybe that'll fix the error. Double lines.

"Yeah, well, we've seen the fruit grow back missing flesh and bone on other people, right? Why not internal organs too?"

I try to draw some more villains while we wait for the doctor. Lacey tells me to stop, and she grabs the pencil and pad. The ultrasound confirms a tiny embryo. The doctor points out various features. The head, the body, a circle that the doctor says is the yolk sac—I didn't know human embryos had yolks. I place my arm around Lacey's shoulders. She asks the doctor about her antidepressants and if she should stop taking them. She asks about sex and if we can still have it. She asks about the sauna and if that's somehow bad for the baby. She asks and she asks, and her hand moves across my sketchpad. I assume she's writing down the doctor's answers, but when she gives it back to me, there are baby names scrawled on the first page. The second page contains a swooping curvilinear sketch of what might've been an obtuse ultrasound. It's a beautiful drawing, like the ones Lacey used to do when we first met, before hysterectomies and Etsy and depression and our golden fruit empire. In her MFA program, her favorite professor always described her artwork as motherly. I'm not sure that my comics could ever be called fatherly.

Lacey puts a copy of the ultrasound on our fridge, next to my farmer Joker sketch. She also frames two copies: one for her attic and one for my Batcave. I take the ultrasound out of the frame and pocket it. In the empty frame, I place

Fruit Rot

Lacey's sketch. The sketch is our child—I can see our baby in the sketch, clearer than the fuzzy blob of an ultrasound.

I go through storage boxes until I find Lacey's old grad school work. I see the same ovals and lines and arcs. I see babies and mothers and fathers and Lacey and me. But mostly, I see love. And I understand why Lacey is happy when she paints, and why fridge magnets had been killing her, and why my failed comics feel like personal deficiencies. I need to create a villain, and soon. I need to write this story before our child is born. It's our story, and it needs a happy ending. A superhero story can't end happily unless the villain is defeated.

I think about cube-like villains to fight the plant-hero-guy and his curvilinear embryonic sidekick. I draw old-school, blocky robots, like Alice from *The Jetsons*. The drawings suck, but I keep sketching, knowing that eventually my lines will form something usable. A loud bang startles me, and my pencil splinters in half. I pull a piece of graphite out of my pinky. It's too dark outside for most of the cameras to pick up anything, but the motion sensors are clean, so it's probably nothing. Still, I feel like I should investigate. This time, I remember to take off the Batsuit first.

I trip over an incapacitated guard, and my knee twists. With my reacquired limp, I hobble to the electrical panel and hit the floodlights. Another incapacitated guard is next to the tree, directly across from a heap of deactivated snares. Another guard is bleeding out while yet another guard cradles his head. "I panicked when I saw the bodies. I switched to live rounds and started shooting. I thought he was the intruder," the guard shouts.

I brush my hands through the dense, sparkling leaves, hoping to find a piece of fruit to save this dying man. There are none within reach. "I need to get the ladder," I say.

"His pulse is dropping fast," the guard tells me. I start to limp away when a woman jumps down from the tree holding a golden fruit in her hand. She's got Kevlar again and some sort of high-tech goggles. Her belt could be mistaken for a fully functional Batbelt with its zippered pouches, several ropes, two grappling hooks, stun gun, compass, and some electronic doodad that I don't recognize.

The high-tech, ninja-like intruder lifts her goggles. I recognize her from earlier—the increasingly wily repeat offender. "I'm sorry. I didn't want your staff to get hurt," she says. She extends her hand.

The guard flinches before realizing that she's offering the golden fruit. He tries to bite it, but he's too weak. His skin loses pigment and his eyes droop, his chapped lips still wrapped around the fruit's unbroken skin. The other guard helps move the man's jawbone, forcing a big bite. I massage the dying man's throat while the woman crouches next to me, pressing her hands on the guard's gunshot wound. Blood bubbles through her fingers. The guard swallows and makes some hoarse noises. The blood stops, and the intruder lifts her fingers. The guard's flesh is pink and new. He opens his eyes. He'll live, thanks to the fruit.

The intruder wipes away the leftover blood and grabs the blackened fruit from the guard's hand. "Thank you," he says to her.

She begins to walk away, and I call out, "Wait, you can't eat the black ones. Please, let me get you a fresh golden one. You deserve it."

"No I don't," she says.

"Yeah you do. You could've just ran off and let him die. You could've gotten away with it. Instead, you gave him the fruit."

"But I don't need a fresh one," she says.

"No, listen," I say. "The rotten ones will kill your whole family."

"I know," she says. She walks toward the fence. I limp beside her.

"You know?"

"Yes. I want the black one. That's all I ever wanted."

She nears the fence as the backup team arrives and encircles her. She stares at me and raises the blackened fruit. The guards inch closer, but I hold up my hand and signal for them to stand down. The woman does not break eye contact as she takes a bite from the diseased, infested flesh. Bugs wiggle around the outside of her mouth while tarry juices slide through her teeth, dripping down her chin as she swallows the rot. She climbs the fence, wriggles through a clipped section of razor-wire, and disappears into the night. I'm not sure why I let her eat the fruit.

I pull the ultrasound photo from my pocket. It's like a storyboard panel, and I see a speck on the edge of the photo. Something faint. A little squiggle that might be a plant-hero-guy. And he's rushing from the edge of my periphery, charging the perimeter and scaling the fence to kill me and take the baby, to save this new child from a lifetime of villains.

The Last Dinosaurs of Portland

Moisés hadn't seen another dinosaur in years. He remembered that allosaurus bully from middle school. There was the stegosaurus at that NOFX show back in '96. The pterodactyl bus driver in his old neighborhood. These whispers of his clade had all but died out amid gentrification and what seemed like a million years of human encroachment. He was a novelty and a vestige of something long gone, and so was this triceratops standing in front of him.

Amy had no memory of other dinosaurs. Not even her parents. She had a few photos. But she couldn't recall feeling them, holding them, being held by them. Even the memory of the memory was gone. If she thought hard enough, she could maybe approach the *idea* of other dinosaurs, but it was entirely based on museum exhibits—all bones and plaster. She had no concept of what her own flesh felt like. She wanted to reach out and touch this tyrannosaurus standing in front of her.

He felt an instant kinship but also a strangeness and hesitation because it'd been so long since he bared his teeth and thundered his voice in conversation with a *real* dinosaur. The triceratops spoke first, easing the tension that he knew was drowning them both: "What brings you here?"

She wanted to ask if he had nightmares too. She wanted to know if he hated humans. She wanted to know if he ever devoured anyone and what they tasted like. She wanted and wanted more. But all she could do was ask "What brings you here?" in her best attempt at casual intonation.

Moisés felt the weight of this question. The accusation that he should have been by her side all along, coupled to the genuine curiosity inherent in the inquiry. This triceratops had suffered in this human city by herself, and he had given up looking for other dinosaurs after the last ankylosaurus was reported dead. He wasn't sure why the ankylosaurus was the tipping point; maybe its armor and veneer of indestructibility had something to do with it. Moisés knew that any of them could be next, and any ideas of a dinosaur collective were long dead and hopeless. His nightmares of heat and pressure and ash were burning brighter. He could almost taste the blood in his mouth every morning.

Amy genuinely wanted to know, but she also hoped he'd reciprocate the question. She needed to tell her story to somebody who might understand. She'd only been in Portland for three months and had already worked her way through the BDSM circuit as both dom and sub to whoever paid the most. She enjoyed taking out her anger on humans. She yearned to stomp them into paste and impale them on her horns, but the typical limit was a simple bone crushing now and then. She also enjoyed having her skin flayed and her appendages jolted with electricity because it was the only way she could feel anything through her thick exterior, seemingly muted and dead to an outside world that never wanted her.

So rather than fight the imminent terror, he ignored it; he kept his head down and did his job. He did whatever he needed to do for a paycheck, only occasionally letting his desire for dinosaur companionship bleed through. There was the meat packing plant for two months. He was fired when a pallet of ground chuck went missing; his jagged tyrannosaur jawline made him guilty without a second thought—never mind that Moisés had gone vegan years earlier.

In her hometown, out in the sticks of Iowa, she had wanted a different future when a formless version of her mother said, "You can do anything if you dream it." She tossed and turned and dreamed about being a doctor or lawyer who one day died in an inferno after some horror fell from the sky. She woke screaming. She woke to a place without her parents. She went to a school that wasn't big enough for dinosaurs, and she was handed an IEP and lessons like, "Here's a BBC documentary on VHS. See you next week."

There was the shipping company that hired him after a five-minute interview; the manager had dreams of tenfold production built on the back of a massive prehistoric creature. The manager assumed trucks would be loaded quicker and cheaper and all for under-the-table, less-than-minimum wages. In actuality, the shipping center's cramped ceiling made it impossible to work. Portland's vocational landscape was entirely humanoid, with its tight doorways and low-weight-bearing joists and delicate levers demanding opposable thumbs. The shipping job lasted three days before Moisés accidentally put his tail through a wall.

She bounced between foster homes. She learned to hate the children who got adopted. Her BBC documentaries weren't enough, and she never graduated. Her small town didn't have a GED program, so she persisted diploma-less. She worked at Blockbuster Video and memorized every line of dialogue in her favorite horror movies. She liked the ones where everybody dies—even the final girl. She took a second job at Domino's and ate pizza every night on the cheap. When that didn't fill her, she devoured any cornfield not fenced or guarded. She used up whatever the small town was willing to give—which wasn't much.

Next, he got a gig at a used car dealership, standing by the I-5 holding a billboard and shouting about the latest deals on used Geo Metros. He had to rotate between different intersections whenever enough public nuisance complaints rolled in. Eventually, he was let go when the dealership realized that junk mail marketing would be cheaper.

When the Blockbuster went bankrupt and the Domino's stopped employing and/or serving dinosaurs, she hit the road. She hitchhiked her way west—like the pioneers of old—riding the backs of semitrucks. She crushed at least one vending machine at every rest stop. She told the truckers about how she was going to star in horror movies one day.

Then there was the roadie position where he lugged speaker cabinets and suitcases full of methamphetamine, and he got *FTW* tattooed on his arm back when *FTW* meant *Fuck the World* instead of *For the Win*. He lived his life according to heavily distorted power chords with intermittent palm muting. He talked about anarchy, and the other roadies talked about how capitalism was to blame for the disappearance of dinosaurs, and for a brief interlude he once again believed that one day dinosaurs might topple the human government. Eventually, the band went on an overseas tour and left him behind—the cargo plane necessary to bring Moisés simply cost too much.

She bought an oversized wig and practiced her best humanoid smile. She never made it far enough down the coast to find out if there was a market for dinosaur actors. She stopped in Portland for a meal at a soup kitchen and found herself breaking somebody's arm in the restroom for twenty bucks and an ounce. She started working the stage at reputable joints like Dante's, but once the patrons had seen one dinosaur, they had seen enough. The shock and awe lasted a hot second, and then she had to go underground. She got a reputation as somebody who could make you feel so much ecstasy that you'd forget you ever had a safe word.

Then there was busking outside of Trader Joe's and selling plasma and eating out of dumpsters. There was his brief stint as a nude model for Portland State University's life drawing class. He dealt weed until it became legal and his hipster clients preferred brightly lit, orchid-lined showrooms to alleys and dive bars.

The money was good. In those past three months, she made enough to rent a warehouse—the walls were temporary, and some rusted millwork equipment remained bolted to the floor—but it was affordable and big enough for her to stretch out, to feel empty space, the air kissing her in ways her clients weren't allowed to.

Job after job, he made rent for a couple months at most; he made workplace friends that vanished within a few days of his termination; he found the best fetid pools to take baths and the nearest all-you-can-eat salad bars that would serve dinosaurs. Until one day, he found himself following a track-marked skinhead who knew a speakeasy hiring dinosaurs for fights and stripteases and shit like that. And here he was, staring at this triceratops that he'd soon battle for spare change and applause and a miniscule cut of anything the bookie brought in.

She secretly still thought that her new life could lead to acting—maybe in a snuff film, but better than nothing. But she didn't tell anybody. Who would she tell anyway? Her clients? She went through friends daily, changing them more often than her various wigs; most people were only interested in *saying* they had a dinosaur friend. When she heard that the speakeasy's dinosaur fights were filmed and distributed on the dark web, she thought maybe a portion of the footage could be usable if she ever wanted to make an acting reel.

"I'm here for the money," Moisés replied, though that was only half true. He felt the hot judgement emanating from this triceratops as he lingered on the word: *Money.* Survival. The two might as well be interchangeable for Moisés, but the response reeked of triviality. "You?"

"I'm here for the money," the t-rex replied. His hoarse, barely audible reply reeked of rotten teeth. "You?" he intoned, his eyes urging for something honest in response, but if he wasn't willing to share the reasons beneath his reasons, Amy didn't feel the need to let down her guard.

"Fame," the triceratops said, though it seemed disingenuous, and a quick look at their pallid surroundings didn't square with her response. Moisés considered calling bullshit, but then he'd feel compelled to be more honest too. He'd need to explain that money was just a façade. Maybe he wanted the chance to sink his teeth into something again with a clear conscience, or maybe he was hoping to lose and die.

"Fame," Amy said. A half-truth to match the t-rex's standoffishness. If he didn't want to let her in, then fuck it. All the humans she ever knew were assholes, why shouldn't this dinosaur be the same? Had he proven the tiniest bit empathetic in this few-word exchange, maybe she would've divulged more. But for now, how could she explain that she wanted to finally kill someone, that the last three months prepared her for this?

Or maybe that was bullshit, and something had summoned him. Something other than the skinhead and his small wad of singles. It was like there was a gravity to this city that had left him behind. Like something was beckoning him to its bloody dinosaur pit. Like it was a nexus of Americana and nostalgia where two prehistoric creatures could become what they once were. They could growl and fight and give into the despair that he knew they both felt. They could surrender to tooth and talon and horn, or they could fight back. They could prove themselves alive and momentarily forget about their nightmares.

Or maybe that was bullshit, and something had summoned her. Something other than the promise of a sample for her reel. It was like there was a gravity to this city that had called her from Iowa. Like something was beckoning her to its bloody dinosaur pit. Like it was a memory of her lost family and a monument where two prehistoric creatures could remember their roots. They could growl and fight and give into the despair that she knew they both felt. They could surrender to tooth and talon and horn, or they could fight back. They could prove themselves alive and momentarily forget about their nightmares.

As Moisés considered how to best phrase this, heat emanated from the moment. It reminded him of a waking version of his ongoing night terrors. The atmosphere warmed, and a sonic boom resonated through the air, and he knew that somewhere on the horizon a meteor was about to strike the earth. He knew exactly what would come next. He snorted air through his mighty nostrils and let out a roar, giving in to a tragedy that was both distant and familiar.

As Amy considered how to best phrase this, heat emanated from the moment. It reminded her of a waking version of her ongoing night terrors. The atmosphere warmed, and a sonic boom resonated through the air, and she knew that somewhere on the horizon a meteor was about to strike the earth. She knew exactly what would come next. She snorted air through her mighty nostrils and let out a roar, giving in to a tragedy that was both distant and familiar.

Kitchenly Perfection

There's a face behind our sink. Scratch that. There's a face behind the tile above our sink. I hope that makes sense. It's hard to describe, really. We chiseled away that old tile, we chipped off countless layers of caked-on grime, and there's this face. Plain as day. Or maybe not plain as day. It's been overcast lately. Plain as a well-lit two-bedroom colonial. There it is. A human face. Scratch that. It's a head. Sort of. It's got dimension to it. It's not like that Shroud of Turin thing. This is a legit face or head or whatever. It has texture. It has smile lines. Crow's feet. Moles. There are a shit-ton of moles—maybe some are melanomas. This face is so lifelike, it's scary. The dude even blinked a few times. He doesn't talk, though.

We're not sure what to do about the face, so we continue our renovations elsewhere, mostly ignoring the face. We rip out the cabinets and replace the trim and change the leaky fixtures and avoid eye contact with the face. We're not heartless, though. We occasionally offer the face sips of water and bites of food, but he never wants any, so we keep to our tasks. We talk in hushed tones even though I don't think the face-person can hear us—his ears are mostly still covered in plaster.

We research the previous owners and learn nothing. Scratch that. We learn something. We learn that this house was owned by a widow. We learn that she was involved in the Underground Railroad. Actually, that gives the wrong impression. I should clarify. This widow was involved in stopping the Underground Railroad. She ratted out all the abolitionists in town. So we did learn that a Civil War-era jackass used to live here. But we didn't learn anything that has to do with this face.

    We take photographs of the face and pass them around town. The flyers start out rather plainly: *Have you seen this man?* and *Do you know this man?* Eventually, our captions grow more desperate: *Why the fuck is this man in our wall?* and *Is this man even a man?* and *Is he alive?* and *Is this some kind of sick joke?*

    We've avoided the inevitable long enough. We pace back and forth in front of the face for hours. We take turns holding the sledgehammer. The rest of our renovations are completely done. The countertops sparkle. The new fridge vibrates gently. The cabinets glide open and closed revealing several lazy Susans and adjustable shelves and special hook thingies for wine glasses. It's all so perfect.

    But the crumbling, naked plaster above our sink lingers. This is the last thing standing in the way of our perfect kitchen. Once we've achieved this kitchenly perfection, everything else will fall into place. I will poach eggs for breakfast. You will bake tarts for dessert. We'll host fancy parties around the center island. We'll laugh into our martini glasses while eating hors d'oeuvres. We'll glue felt on the bottoms of all our kitchen chairs so we don't scratch the new hardwood floors. We'll wipe down the stove after every use like the manufacturer recommends. We'll brush our teeth in the kitchen sink for good measure. But we won't do any of those things with a face behind our sink, or behind the wall above the sink, or wherever. This kitchen is everything. This is what will make us love one another. We both sense it. Without this kitchen, we are just two strangers fucking in the dark.

We inspect the mole-covered face one last time. He still doesn't speak. He blinks once. Nothing else. We tell each other that the face-person must be brain-dead. We tell each other that he won't feel a thing. We tell each other that it's our wall and we can demolish it if we please. We tell each other everything we want to hear.

Three-Month Autopsy

"Why do you have your ex's heart?" I asked, holding up a mason jar with *Manuel* scrawled on its lid. The sickly heart kept an irregular beat, flopping around inside the jar as if dancing to polyrhythmic jazz. The heart had several dark lesions on it—probably something a doctor should've looked at.

"What, like you don't have anything like that from an ex?" Ravi replied.

"I have Jay's stomach and Desmond's liver. But this is different. This is his *heart*," I said.

"You're just buying into greeting card propaganda. A heart is no different than a stomach or liver or whatever. It's just an organ. It moves blood around the body. Big deal. It's not like a heart has anything to do with love."

"Does he have *your* heart?" I asked.

"No, of course not. My heart belongs to you," Ravi said.

"Yeah, right. Now who's been reading too many greeting cards?"

"No, I'm serious," he said.

"Prove it," I said.

Ravi sighed and walked into the kitchen. I followed him. He retrieved a chef's knife from a drawer. He jammed the blade into his sternum until his chest cavity opened with a pop and a gurgle. "See, all yours," Ravi said, pointing to his heart *thump*, *thump*, *thumping* away in the open space. The deep, vibrant red muscle churned blood at precise intervals—nothing like the dejected, ruined thing in the mason jar.

"Okay, then give it to me," I demanded, pulling an empty Pyrex container from the cabinet.

"Wait a minute. We've only been dating for three months," Ravi protested.

"You said it's mine, so I want it," I said.

"It's more like an expression," he said.

"Not for Manuel it isn't," I shouted, wiggling the mason jar. The mottled heart smooshed against the glass and stopped beating for a few seconds.

"Listen, you can have my heart someday. But that's months down the road."

"Okay, when? How many months?"

"You're asking me to put a timeline on something like that?"

"This isn't just a casual thing for me. If this isn't going anywhere, then I want to know now."

"Alright, alright. How about another three months? Once we've been together a half-year, then I'll rip out my heart for you."

"Okay, deal," I said. "In the meantime, I don't think you should be holding onto an ex-lover's heart. You gotta give this back to Manuel." I placed the jar on the counter and slid it to Ravi.

"Fair enough. But then you need to give back the stomach and the liver. I don't think it's fair for *either* of us to have these prior attachments."

"They aren't attachments. They're—" I stopped myself before explaining my rationale. Ravi was right, or at least he was half-right. I still thought that the heart was more important than other body parts, but if we wanted a future together, then we couldn't keep any of these old pieces of our exes. Heart, stomach, liver. It all needed to go. This was about us now. "Okay, that's fair. I'll give back the stomach and the liver this weekend."

———

Jay had moved out of their studio apartment. The post office woman gave me their forwarding address, though I'm not sure if she was technically supposed to—she gave me a wink at the end of our exchange. Jay's new place looked like something out of campy seventies sci-fi. Everything was white and clean and sterile. Their furniture had that retro mod look while still being somewhat strange and futuristic.

"I never minded that you still had my stomach. I knew you'd take good care of it. You were always such a good cook," they told me while sipping from a wide saucer of Earl Grey tea. "But I suppose if it's making your lover—what was his name? Ravi?"

"Yeah, Ravi."

"If it's making *Ravi* uncomfortable, then sure, I'll take it back. I just don't know what I'll *do* with it," Jay said. They looked at the stomach sloshing around inside a Ziploc bag. "Mel is terrible in the kitchen," they added.

"Thanks. It means a lot to me. It's not that I don't like your stomach—it's just the best way for Ravi and me to move forward. You know?"

"Oh, I hear you. Mel had a whole collection of ex-lover body parts. There were nineteen in all. *Nineteen.* Can you believe it? I put a stop to that right away. Then we each agreed to give up our ears, and we've been together ever since," they said. They pulled back a clump of shaggy hair, revealing a sunken crater where their left ear used to be. "Mel is such a good listener."

"Wait, so you *each* gave up an ear?" I glanced around the room, expecting the dual ears to be on display somewhere.

"Yes. The left ear. Both of us. Full Van Gogh."

"How does that work, though? Having two people who are good listeners?" I asked. I thought about Ravi, and how he seemed like a good listener, but not a good sharer. I never knew what he was thinking. When I prodded for a direct opinion, he'd always say, *I dunno*, with a shrug. Or if he felt like being a smartass, he'd say, *I'm thinking about stuff*. So our communication wasn't always mutual, but I was grateful to have somebody I could vent to. He was like a vault, ready to receive my problems and lock them away.

"It works just fine for us," Jay said with a scowl. "You can be a good listener even if your partner isn't a talker. Sometimes we just sit and stare at each other, and we listen to our body language. We listen to our rhythms. We listen to our hearts beating."

I hadn't told Jay about the heart, but I considered it in that moment. I wondered what this person with their sterile life and double-listener relationship might say about it. I wondered if they'd understand why I was sensitive about the heart. If Jay was *really* such a good listener, would they listen to me? During our time together, they didn't strike me as particularly good at listening. But in that moment, as I mulled over these thoughts, they placed their tea on a coaster and folded their hands, patiently giving space for me to say my piece. I wanted to snatch their one remaining ear and take it for myself.

"Can I ask you something?" I finally said.

"Of course," they said. I appreciated the softness in that simple response—the delicacy with my concern. Ravi might've said, *You just did ask me something*.

"Why didn't you ever ask for anything from me? Like my ear or whatever?"

"Oh," they said, leaning back in their chair. "I guess I didn't know where we stood. I didn't know if we were compatible."

"Because I'm not a good listener?"

"No, not that." Jay waved their hands dismissively. "You were a good listener. Your ears were fine. I actually took a piece of your lobe one night when we were watching a movie together."

"What?" I exclaimed. I began touching both my ears, searching for any missing flesh.

Jay laughed. "I put it back right way. I only held onto it for fifteen minutes." They folded their hands again and spoke slower. "Here's the honest truth. You were good at listening. You were good at cooking. You were good at a lot of things. But you weren't *great* at anything."

"What's that supposed to mean?"

"That came out wrong," they said. "This is why I'm a listener and not a talker. Let me explain. There wasn't anything I wanted from you. Not long-term anyway. We had fun. But it was a fling."

"Okay, I guess that's true," I said, but only because I didn't want to argue or take the conversation down an awkward path. The way *I* remembered it, we were more than a fling. In my mind, Jay was stable. They were a long-term lover—a partner. Sure, we didn't have an uncanny connection where we sat and listened to nothingness for hours, but we had our own type of stability—buttoned-down and tame and safe. They were my comfortable lover. Their life was so orderly that they had *always* decorated their home with a theme—before this seventies sci-fi vibe, their old studio apartment had been a curated collection of hipster bohemian chic, right out of some glossy lifestyle magazine. Jay's life was full of order and careful design. If I could've had any body part, it would've been their analytical brain. I don't know how the hell I wound up with their stomach.

As Jay took another sip of Earl Grey in silence, I considered cracking their head like a coconut and scooping out the insides. But what would Mel say when arriving back home? What would I say to Ravi? This part of my life was over. That's what the entire visit was supposed to be about. Closure. I reminded myself: *You're just here to give back the stomach. You're just here to give back the stomach. You're just here to give back the stomach.* I think I said it out loud once, or maybe Jay was so good at reading body language that they sensed my internal monologue. "I know why you're here. I'll make sure this finds a good home. Maybe Mel and I can take a cooking class together." Jay walked off with the Ziploc bag. I waited for nearly ten minutes before I let myself out.

Desmond kicked a pile of unopened junk mail off the coffee table and propped his feet up. He still shared the rickety four-bedroom with something like ten other guys. Back when Desmond and I dated, it had a frat vibe to it. The place was still a pigsty, but the mess had morphed into a staging area for young professionals. Hung above the floor-bound clutter were racks of freshly pressed suits. Stacks of glossy magazines had been transformed into stacks of hardcover books about *leadership* and *disrupting the paradigm*. The messy kitchen paired unwashed dishes alongside several containers of fresh fruit and vegetables, as if food were being prepared rather than simply reheated or reconstituted from freeze-dried packages. Perhaps most tellingly, there wasn't a single empty beer can anywhere—when Desmond and I dated, all we did was party.

"So you're doing a relationship autopsy, huh?" he said.

"No, that's not it," I said.

"Yes, it is. You want to see why we broke up. You want to give back that liver and then talk about why we failed."

"I know why we failed. This isn't about us. This is about Ravi and me having a fresh start with no baggage."

"Uh huh, sure," he said. He held the Ziploc baggy under a nearby lamp. "Did my liver always look like this?" He poked the shriveled gray and black thing.

"Probably not. We drank all the time. I think that's how I ended up with your liver."

"Ended up with? You stole it," Desmond announced.

"No, I didn't. If anything, you tried to take mine," I said. I instinctively held my hands over my abdomen, as if he might still be tempted to grab a knife and snatch my liver at any moment. I couldn't believe that he was blaming me for the loss of his liver. He was the party animal, not me.

"Maybe. But I think you're looking at this with a holier-than-thou tint," he said.

"What does that mean?"

"It means that we were young. We had that messy, passionate, fiery young love that makes people crazy. We partied. That was us. That was our relationship. There wasn't much substance beyond that. I barely drank before we met."

"Bullshit. *I* barely drank before we met. *You* were the drinker. Don't pin your diseased liver on me."

"I'm not pinning anything on you. We're doing a relationship autopsy, remember?" He slid forward, nearly falling out of his chair, his eyes wide with excitement.

"You're nuts. You have your liver. I'm leaving," I said.

"I didn't mean it like that. Stay for another few minutes. Seriously, I want to help. What's going on with this Ravi guy? Are you happy?"

"Yeah, of course," I said.

Desmond smirked as if he had just discovered a bombshell. His follow-up question was less intense than I expected. "Here's the real test. Do you still love him when you're just watching TV or reading a book? Is that enough for you?"

"I don't think that's the real test. The real test is more like figuring out how we both might handle a crisis together."

Desmond evaded the rebuttal and changed course. "Why are you suddenly giving me this liver after all these years?" he asked.

I considered bolting for the door again, but some part of me wanted to talk about it. I wondered if Desmond could give me more insight. If Jay was the listener, maybe Desmond was the talker. Maybe he could blurt out the things that I needed to hear. I sat back down. "Okay, so here's the deal—" I proceeded to tell Desmond about Manuel's heart and Ravi's three-month timeline. I don't know why I felt safe divulging all those details. In part, I think it was because Desmond and I had no mutual friends. Even if he was untrustworthy, there wasn't much risk of this conversation getting back to Ravi or anybody else I knew. Desmond had given up his liver years ago—he knew what it was like to sacrifice a body part—I needed to hear the rationale. I asked him why Ravi might be hesitant to give me his heart, and I asked if that was a bad sign for our relationship.

"Yeah, that's a bad sign, but not for the reasons you think," he responded immediately, almost before I finished speaking. "The fact that Ravi didn't give you his heart is meaningless. Nobody wants to give up something like their heart. You think I was happy about this?" He poked the diseased liver again.

"It's not my fault—"

Desmond cut me off before I could protest further. "I know. We've been over that. It's nobody's fault." He paused for a moment. "Okay, here's the thing. My heart isn't in here anymore," he said, tapping his sternum. "One of my exes has it. You know why? It's not because I *gave* the heart to him. It's because he *took* it. That's how it works."

"I don't think that's how it works," I said.

"No, trust me. That's how it works. So Ravi took some guy's heart years ago. So what? People fall in love. They fall out of love. Shit happens. But here's where it gets bad for you. Ravi *showed* you his heart, and you didn't take it," Desmond said.

"Yeah, so?"

"It was there, beating right in front of you, and you didn't take it. *That* is your bad sign. I remember when I lost mine. It was snapped up so fast that I didn't have a chance. I also took a different heart a few years back, and it was the same thing. I just grabbed it on impulse. If you really wanted Ravi's heart, it'd be yours by now. I think it's *you* who is not in this relationship one hundred percent. That's what I mean by holier-than-thou. This is more your issue than Ravi's. You gotta figure out what you really want in that relationship."

"Oh really? What do you know about it?" I stormed out. On the bus ride home, I considered my earlier visit with Jay and how I wanted their ear and their brain. I could almost feel my hands twitching into action. I admired parts of them. I respected those parts. Maybe I even loved those parts. What did I love about Ravi? What did I want to take?

―――

When I met Ravi that evening, our dinner reservation wasn't for another two hours. I went inside and made myself a cocktail. The heart was no longer on the counter. In its place, Ravi had put a framed picture of us. It seemed a little too spot-on, like he was trying too hard to appease me after our bickering match.

"I assume you saw Manuel today?" I called out.

"Yeah," Ravi said, hurrying into the room. "You like what I've done with the place?" He motioned to the picture.

"Yeah, really classes up the joint," I said with the most over-the-top sarcastic tone possible.

"You okay?" he asked.

"Yeah, I'm fine. But I was thinking. Can I see your heart again, just one time?"

"I don't know. It's not exactly—"

"Please—" I did my best hangdog expression. "I promise I won't bring it up again until the three months are up."

"Sure, I guess. Why not." He grabbed a knife.

"Do you think hearts are given or taken?" I asked. I considered Desmond's philosophy, and I considered how Jay briefly took a piece of my lobe.

"I don't know." He slid the blade into the unhealed slit from earlier.

"Yeah, me neither," I said. I approached and wiggled my fingers, ready to snatch his heart the moment it presented itself.

Ravi rotated the knife and popped open his chest cavity. Inside the bloody chasm, Ravi's healthy, robust heart had been swapped with Manuel's grotesque little thing. I don't know how Ravi thought I wouldn't notice. There was no way this imposter heart could pass for his. The diseased thing thumped at irregular intervals. Its dark spots pulsed and shimmied with the excitement of new blood, and I had my answer.

The Elevator Elf

The maintenance access hatch in the elevator's ceiling opened, and an elf poked his head out. At least I think he was an elf. He was rather small and had those pointy elf ears, but his skin was green and leathery and perhaps goblin-like. I'm not so sure about the exact definitions of these things—I'm more into sci-fi than fantasy. The elevator elf held a three-hole punch in his left hand. "Where's Chris?" he asked.

"He quit yesterday," I said.

The elf frowned. "Who are you?"

"I'm Brian."

The elevator elf inspected the three-hole punch as if he'd never seen one before. "This won't do you any good. Let me check my list." The elf disappeared through the elevator hatch. He returned a moment later holding a ballpoint pen. "Here," he said, thrusting the pen at me.

I took the pen. Before I could ask what to do with it, the elf disappeared into the ceiling, and the maintenance hatch slammed shut. The elevator dinged and the doors opened. I backed out of the elevator, keeping my eyes on the unassuming hatch the entire time. I bumped into Kasper, and he spilled his coffee.

I worked on the Teschner file. Then I sent out a series of redundant emails to HR, marketing, and my boss, informing everybody that the numbers looked good, and we could close the deal tomorrow.

Just before lunch, I popped into Dakota's cubicle while she muttered something to herself. "What's wrong?" I asked.

"The supply closet isn't stocked again. Kasper forgot to order pens, and all mine are dead." She threw a dried-up pen aside, joining a pile of other rejected writing utensils. "This place is so dysfunctional."

"I have a pen," I said.

She looked up from her inkless scribbling. "Can I have it?" she whispered. She looked around, as if we were discussing some clandestine dossier.

"Sure," I said.

"Thanks," she said. She began to sign various forms and scrawl memos across company letterhead. Dakota was one of the few people in the office who still handwrote everything. She always had an old-school vibe to her work. She recorded meetings on cassettes rather than a laptop. She stapled her paperwork by hand, even though the copy machine had an automatic stapler built into it. She even still used carbon copies, filing everything in triplicate on corresponding white, yellow, and pink slips. This nostalgic charm was one of the reasons I liked her.

I walked away, but I caught her muttering to herself as I left. "That Brian is always so nice."

The next morning, the elevator elf appeared again. "How did you know about the pen?" I asked.

The elf didn't respond. He furrowed his brow and blinked incessantly. After a few more seconds of blinking, he handed me a USB flash drive. I wanted to say thanks, but he was gone before I could.

The Teschner people showed up early, and the presentation in Conference Room B wasn't ready. "Why the hell didn't anybody put the PowerPoint in the cloud?" Larry shouted.

"We still have the graphs," Kasper said, motioning toward several easels containing poorly saturated pie charts. He framed each one with his hands, like Vanna White on *Wheel of Fortune*.

"Nobody gives a damn about graphs," Larry said. "PowerPoint is where it's at. That's what makes a good presentation. And transitions. The ones with those floaty things and smooth dissolves." He gazed out the window as if he could see the smooth dissolves waiting for him on some distant landscape.

"How much time do we have to slap a presentation together?" the boss asked, finally breaking his stoicism. Nobody answered because doing so might incur hellfire. Realistically, time was short. Dakota was distracting the Teschner people with an office tour, but there wasn't much to see. Some dead ferns, a poorly stocked supply room, and a pile of gutted computers in Conference Room A. The computer shells had been sitting there ever since a freak power surge fried half the office a few years ago—the IT guys yanked all the salvageable components after the crash. Since then, there had been meetings about cleaning out Conference Room A, but nobody could agree on which department should be responsible for the mess.

"Fuck!" the boss screamed. "This is the most important meeting of the year, and nobody backs up the damn PowerPoint?"

Everybody joined in, sharing the boss's frustration and hoping to deflect blame: "Dammit!" "Fuck." "Shit sandwich."

"I have a backup," I announced. I offered the trinket to the group, cupping it in both hands like a treasure.

"Thank heavens," Larry said. He stretched his huge arms around me and gave a crushing hug.

Larry browsed the drive while the projector powered up. Sure enough, my gamble paid off—the elevator elf had given me a goldmine. The flash drive was loaded with endless files labeled "Teschner Presentation - Draft 1," Teschner Presentation - Draft 2" and so on, until finally topping out at "Teschner Presentation - Draft 99 (Final)." Larry opened it and scrolled through the fantastic graphics and dazzling transitions.

"Nice work," the boss said.

The Teschner people were impressed, and we landed the account. Hollywood-style over-exaggerated high fives all around. We all knew Christmas bonuses were in order, and mine would be fatter than the rest.

The following day, the elevator elf gave me some matches and a stick of gum. Dakota popped into my cubicle over lunch. "I heard that you saved the meeting yesterday," she said.

"Not really," I said.

"But it would've fallen apart without the PowerPoint. That was the clincher."

"Maybe," I said, partly out of modesty, partly because Larry's lust for smooth dissolves wasn't universal—I didn't think that the PowerPoint really mattered.

There was a long silence. I reached into my pockets and considering giving her the matches or the gum, but I wasn't sure why. The elevator elf gave me the trinkets for a reason—it just hadn't presented itself yet.

"Did the Teschner people like the graphs too?" Dakota asked.

"Yeah, I think so," I said, though I wasn't sure.

"I made those graphs, you know."

"Oh, they were very nice graphs."

"You think my graphs are sexy?" she asked.

I wasn't sure if this was office flirtation. Who the hell thinks graphs are sexy? I had no idea how to respond.

"Relax," she said. "I was kidding."

I forced a laugh.

She lifted a boxy red purse onto my desk and began rummaging through it. "Dammit," she said. "Where is it?"

I considered my pockets again. I decided to go for it. "Do you need a light?"

"Yes, how did you know?"

I shrugged.

"Want to join me?" she asked.

I nodded.

The cigarette tasted worse than I remembered cigarettes tasting. It was like sucking on a tailpipe, or licking a dirty stovetop, or some combination of the two. I coughed and clacked my tongue against the roof of my mouth.

"I don't normally smoke," she said. "But I'm stressed out and pissed at my boyfriend. Well, ex-boyfriend, I guess. Chris from HR. Do you know him? Well, he just up and left a couple days ago. Poof. Thin air. He took all his stuff from my apartment and split. Hasn't been to work since. Grapevine says he quit."

"Oh, sorry to hear that," I said. But I wasn't sorry. I didn't know she was dating Chris, but if I had known, I would've hated the guy's guts, and I would've secretly celebrated his departure. Maybe that was a shitty thing to think, especially since Dakota almost cried as we smoked, but at least I was honest with myself. Shitty, but honest.

"Thanks for listening," she said. She stamped out her cigarette, and I did the same, even though I had half of mine left.

I clacked my tongue again and decided the gum might help combat the ashen flavor. "Oh, can I have a piece?" Dakota asked.

"Sure," I said, handing over the only stick in my possession. I spent the rest of the day by the water cooler, covertly gargling in an attempt to wash down unseen tar residue. The taste lingered. Even after lunch, my mouth hadn't returned to normalcy.

    Larry stopped by and congratulated me on the PowerPoint for the billionth time. I had spent months running the Teschner numbers—I even reworked the ordering system to get us a three percent bump on the back end—but all anybody seemed to care about was the PowerPoint. I guess most people are visual learners, and flashy transitions are better than numbers. "You're very welcome," I said, clack-clack-clacking my tongue between each syllable.

    The following day, the elevator elf gave me a lozenge for Dakota's sore throat—an extension of yesterday's cigarette. I wish he'd given me two, but he disappeared as quickly as usual, and I didn't get a chance to ask.

    On Friday, he gave me a safety pin, and I offered it to Kasper when the button fly on his khakis failed. He was embarrassed but appreciative.

    After the weekend, the elevator elf gave me three cupcakes. When Wanda's birthday cake ran out, I produced the treats—just enough for the three hungry IT guys who hadn't gotten a slice. I was the hit of the party, and the IT guys promised to take the porn filter off my computer. "You're one of us now," they said. For an instant, I felt like IT was an exclusive honor rather than a dysfunctional, underpaid cohort who approached most troubleshooting with the same suggestion: "Did you try rebooting?"

    I soon got a reputation as the most well-prepared, well-organized guy in the office. I had a trinket for every situation, and the boss used terms like "go-getter." I helped everybody in the office with some small thing here or there, and I used these occasions to strike up more conversations with Dakota. We talked about whatever was on her mind.

Ex-boyfriend baggage came up a lot. But she also talked about silent films. And ballroom dancing. And her favorite books—mostly obscure Victorian era stuff that I never heard of, way outside the standard Lit 101 realm of the Brontë sisters. "Brontë is for chumps," she'd say. Her favorite Victorian-era book was only available at one specific library in England; it was written by some guy with a French-sounding name, and visitors needed special gloves to handle the pages. She hoped to visit England specifically for this book. From what I could tell, duplicate copies didn't exist, so I wasn't sure how she knew this unread masterpiece was truly her favorite.

Even though she dominated most conversations, I didn't mind. I enjoyed learning all about her. But whenever I felt like flipping the tables, she was patient. My rants about video games and sci-fi were as foreign to her as *The Great Victorian Novel* by Pepé Le Pew was to me, but she actually asked questions and seemed genuinely interested.

After a month of trinkets, the elevator elf gave me a big bouquet of flowers, and I immediately knew what they were for. As soon as I walked into the office, Dakota pointed to the flowers and asked, "Did you get those for me?"

She slipped a note into my pocket, it contained her number and some bad attempt at flirting—a stapler pun about the *Swing* in *Swingline*. There was black, powdery residue on the backside of the paper—I think she carbon copied the note.

For our first date, we went to see a silent film at some artsy theater downtown. It was hard to read the on-screen captions before they disappeared, but I got the gist from the action scenes. These swashbuckling pirates with waxed moustaches kidnapped a girl in a white dress, and this sailor guy in a poofy shirt rescued her. This poofy-shirted hero paddled into the open ocean on a little dinghy, all to rescue his damsel. Heroic stuff, I guess. Way better than gum or lozenges.

I walked her home afterward. She kissed me goodnight. I was thinking about asking to come upstairs, but the elevator elf hadn't given me a condom, so I was pretty sure it wasn't going to happen tonight. "Do you want to go out again next weekend?" I asked.

"Sure," she said. "Maybe we can do something you'll enjoy. Do arcades still exist?"

"Not really. But we could see a non-silent movie. Maybe something sci-fi."

"Okay, sounds fun."

Just before that second date, the elevator elf gave me an umbrella, a new book of matches, and this time he gave me a box of condoms. On the way back from the sci-fi flick, there was a sudden downpour. The umbrella was the perfect size to shelter us, but only if Dakota clung to my body—the elevator elf must've selected a smallish umbrella on purpose, knowing that we'd both welcome the excuse to get close. I could feel her warmth against me. We walked as an intertwined unit, right up to her doorknob. She grabbed my wrist and pulled me inside. She lit candles using my matchbook. She put on a cassette recording of a work meeting; then she apologized and flipped over the tape, blaring a smooth jazz mix. She clapped and her lights turned off—pure nostalgia, like everything she did.

We ordered several meals' worth of Chinese food, stocking Dakota's fridge with lo mein so we wouldn't need to leave her apartment all weekend. I went home just once to get fresh clothes. I also took the opportunity to answer work emails. Even though Dakota had a computer, checking email was difficult on her clunky PC—it still ran Windows 95 on a 56k dial-up modem, and it reminded me of the obsolete computer casings strewn around Conference Room A. My inbox was flooded with messages about weekly Z-612 reports. I purged the inbox and returned to Dakota's apartment. I'd

The Elevator Elf

get chastised for forgetting to file the report, but I had enough goodwill around the office to smooth that over.

We watched silent films on VHS, then I acquainted Dakota with the magic of laptops and streaming video—naturally, she'd heard of things like YouTube and Netflix, but she hadn't actually used them. The next door neighbor's unsecured WiFi connection was sluggish, but we managed to watch *Robocop* and *Robocop II* without much interruption.

We walked to work as a couple. Thankfully, she wanted to take the stairs. I rode the elevator and waited for my next trinket. The hatch opened and the elevator elf popped his head through. "You're late," he scolded.

"Yeah, but you probably knew I would be, didn't you?" I said. I still wasn't sure what he could foresee and what he couldn't—and prodding my benefactor wasn't a great idea—but I felt like we had a rapport now. We almost never spoke, but our strange arrangement seemed to bond us.

The elevator elf rubbed his forehead, and he did his usual rapid blinking. Then he closed his eyes and breathed deep, like he was waiting for me to say something else. "Here," he said. A huge stack of binders and loose paper descended through the elevator hatch. It landed with a clunk. It was the largest elevator item I'd ever seen—even bigger than the bouquet or the umbrella.

"What is all that?" I asked. The elevator elf was already gone, and the elevator hatch slammed shut.

I paged through the first binder. There were a series of proposals and reports, complete with detailed cost/benefit analysis write-ups, a marketing plan, estimated revenue streams for nearly a goddamn decade, and appendices with numbers way beyond my mid-range accounting background—the equations looked like something Stephen Hawking might struggle to understand. "Holy shit," I said to myself.

I dumped the binders and papers on my boss's desk, and I became second-in-command by the day's end. My exact title contained at least three of the following words in variable order depending on who you asked: "Executive," "Innovation," "Director," "Sales," "Marketing," "Business," "Management," and "Chief." I wasn't entirely sure what I was supposed to do in this new, vaguely defined post. All I knew was that my paycheck was larger, and the elevator elf would take care of anything else I needed to succeed.

The elevator elf gave me new cufflinks and a tie clip to impress the Larson reps. He gave me a box of Cuban cigars to pass around the office when the boss announced that his wife had given birth. He gave me staplers and ledgers. He gave me tape dispensers and water bottles. He gave me calculators and paper clips and soap and shoelaces and a turkey sandwich. One day, he gave me a slip of paper with *Patti O'Malley* written on it. When I got to my office that day, three interview candidates awaited. I hired Patti without a second thought and took the rest of the day off.

Gradually, the items became more impressive, dwarfing the initial awe of ballpoint pens or PowerPoint slides. The elevator elf presented me with blueprints for a redesigned office foyer. He gave me the prepaid invoice for ergonomic office chairs. He gave me brand new next-gen computers to replace the broken units in Conference Room A, earning me additional points with the IT guys. One day, he even provided a gigantic new copier—I don't know how it fit through the small elevator hatch. I was just tying my shoelaces in the elevator, then this behemoth machine crashed from above.

Gifts for Dakota became more extravagant too. Tickets to Broadway shows, and then tickets to artsy off-Broadway shows full of off-Brontë references. An old timey film projector and a crate full of original silent film reels. A case of expensive champagne to celebrate our three-month anniversary. The deed to a condo and a beautifully worded letter asking Dakota to move in with me—the elevator elf's handwriting mimicry was uncanny. Finally, a little box containing an engagement ring, plane tickets to England, a hotel voucher, and an exclusive VIP tour of the rare book collection containing Dakota's favorite book. During the trip, she spent something like ten hours delicately paging through that Victorian masterpiece. She would've sneezed on it and gotten us both kicked out, but the elevator elf gave me some Kleenex the day before we left.

In a few months, I'd gone from a nondescript cubical drone to practically running the place, wooing Dakota, making friends with everybody else, and hoarding a sizable bank account to boot. More months flew by as the elevator elf dropped all manner of wedding plans through the hatch, ranging from invitations, to seating charts, to a rather dapper tuxedo. I was a little wary when he dropped down a 1920s flapper-style wedding dress—Dakota had insisted that she didn't want me involved with the dress—but the elevator elf had never steered me wrong before. When I showed her the dress, she cried and said, "It's exactly what I had in mind. It's perfect. How did you—? It's perfect." She repeated to herself a few more times, "Perfect. Perfect. Perfect."

In time, I stopped looking up. I stopped feeling anything but expectant. I walked into the elevator, checking email on my phone or playing something on my vintage Gameboy. I kept my eyes diverted while I held out my hand. The weight of the day's item occasionally caught me off-guard—and the elevator elf was considerate enough to drop extremely large, bone-crushing items away from my outstretched limb—but I was never without a gift. The arrangement had become routine.

Then one day, there was nothing. The elevator doors dinged, and my hand was empty. Kasper waved at me and sauntered forward. "Uh, I forgot something in my car," I said. I rode the elevator back down and glared at the hatch. Nothing.

I locked myself in my office, afraid to make any decisions without the elevator elf's daily gift. I skipped a conference call, unsure if the elf's missing gift would've been notecards with talking points—I didn't want to make a fool of myself without the elf's guidance. I shut myself in my office. I investigated my inbox, looking for clues. Kasper mentioned something about running a few days behind on the L-PQA forms—maybe the elf would've given me those. Dakota sent an email about linens for the wedding—I couldn't tell the difference between the sky blue and robin's egg blue, and maybe the elevator elf would've dropped down a sample swatch of the correct color. There was something about the IT department installing new anti-malware. Wanda's son was selling candy to raise money for camp. The boss sent me a message about a softball game next weekend. Any of these things were potential time bombs. Without the elevator elf's daily assistance, I was destined to make a fool of myself in tiny increments.

Dakota popped in with her earmuffs and MC Hammer-inspired jacket on, ready to go out for our usual lunch break. "I have work to do," I said, waving my hand at her.

"Since when? We always get lunch."

"Not today. Please. Work. Talk later," I said. I flipped through an empty rolodex, hoping it'd make me look busy enough.

"Okay. Love you," she said.

Once Dakota left the building, I rode the elevator up and down nearly a dozen times. Larry's cube was close by, and

The Elevator Elf

he eventually held the door and asked, "Is this thing on the fritz? You need to get off?"

"No, just going down," I said, pushing him back outside. The elevator elf never appeared.

I told Dakota that I needed to stay late. She kissed my cheek. "Okay. Don't work yourself to death." She rode her bike back to our condo. I watched her go from my office window, and I wondered if the elevator elf was supposed to give me a bike helmet that day. I dialed the condo's landline and asked Dakota to call me the minute she got in.

I went to the janitor's closet and retrieved any tool half-resembling a crowbar. I tried to jimmy open the elevator hatch and break into the elevator elf's mysterious world. After an hour of desperate prodding, I hadn't even scratched the hatch's glossy surface. I packed the tools and returned them to the closet.

Dakota called me as I rode the elevator down. "What's going on? Are you sure everything's okay?" she asked.

"Yeah, just don't leave the condo tonight. We'll order in. Okay?"

"Sure, but you'll have to tell me what's going on sooner or later. Can we look at those linen samples when you get home?"

"No. Let's just go to bed early. I've had a long day. I need to relax. I just want to sit and do absolutely nothing."

The elevator hatch lifted slightly—barely a half-inch—and a single sheet of paper slid out. I hung up without saying goodbye.

I began reading the document. I felt as unsure as I had been that first day, handed a simple ballpoint pen from some unfamiliar creature, unaware that it was the first trinket on a path that would change my life. Full of hope, but also apprehension.

The words *embezzlement* and *fraud* stood out. I crumpled the paper and wanted to scream. More papers fell from the hatch. I recognized some of the Stephen Hawking math from months ago, and some random invoice pages, misfiled Z-612 forms, and even some wedding receipts. Yellow highlighter and big red circles covered half the pages with *misappropriation* scribbled in thick ink. I hit the *Stop Elevator* button and began reading more evidence. I saw how all my seemingly magical good fortune could be linked to real-world bank accounts and hedge funds. But I also saw the skill in it. I saw how I wouldn't get caught unless somebody with access to these files spoke out. I began tearing up the papers even as duplicates began sprinkling down, blanketing the elevator in thick clumps. Endless, damning testimony.

Several manila envelopes preaddressed to Dakota fell. Inside, there was a background check stapled to Patti's new-hire paperwork showing felony convictions for corporate fraud. There were hotel receipts and salacious letters and joint bank accounts full of stolen funds—all riddled with my handwriting, mimicked perfectly by the elf. More papers with highlighted evidence and *accomplice* scrawled in red.

I told myself that maybe I could close the elevator for repairs. Maybe I could burn it. But the elevator elf seemed to have a strangely broad reach—how else could he have arranged so much of my wedding, doctored so many bank accounts? Would an all-consuming fire even matter?

The fluttering paper ceased almost as suddenly as it came. The hatch remained barely ajar. I tried to see inside but couldn't. A photograph slipped through the crack. The photo depicted a creature that looked a lot like the elevator elf, except the ears were a little longer and the skin was a brighter shade of green. The elf in the photo flashed a huge grin and held up a wine glass as if making a toast. I flipped the photo

The Elevator Elf

over. The backside included a strange-sounding name and an address just down the street from my condo.

The elevator hatch opened wider for a moment, and the nearby fluorescent lighting reflected a glint of steel. A Clint Eastwood-style six shooter landed near me with a thud, and the elevator hatch slammed shut. The gun's ammunition chamber was glowing. I swung out the cylinder and found it loaded with clear bullets containing a bluish liquid. The substance in these special elf-killing bullets flickered and swirled like fairy dust in a Disney film.

I closed the cylinder and studied the photo of the happy little elf once more, my potential downfall still littered in heaps around me. The elevator elf said something, dampened by the thick hatch so it was almost a whisper: "Now it's your turn. Just do this one thing for me, and I can make it all go away."

Physical Therapy

After four weeks of physical therapy, Oliver's knee wasn't getting any better. He still woke with pain every day, and a steady throb lulled him to sleep. Every time he moved, the joint buckled. The tendons slipped over each other, twisted like drunkards. No noticeable improvement, despite the physical therapist's insistence that "Your range of motion is so much better" or "Your balance is good today" or other unquantifiable bullshit.

The therapist pretended to listen to Oliver's concerns, then set him up on the same exercise machine from the previous session—a stupid pulley system that put stress in all the wrong places. "It may be uncomfortable, but that means the exercises are working." More bullshit.

Oliver tangled himself in the contraption while the physical therapist welcomed another patient. Oliver hadn't seen the guy before, but he was cute. Maybe a little too corporate-looking—gelled hair, nice shoes, gold watch—but still not bad. The physical therapist gave the new guy some tiny dumbbells and showed him a couple overhead maneuvers. The cute guy winced and rubbed his left shoulder. Oliver finished on the weird pulleys and walked over. "Hey, surgery or injury?" he asked.

"Injury. AC joint separation," the guy said. He looked upward, avoiding eye contact. Oliver leaned against the wall to take some weight off his knee.

"I've got tendon damage. Poor patellar tracking. A couple pins. The works," Oliver said.

"Oh, okay," the guy mumbled.

"So who's your doctor?" Oliver asked.

"I don't know. Dr. M-something."

"Mollrich?"

"Sure."

"Me too!" Oliver was excited for some common ground. He sprung from his position on the wall, eager to discuss Dr. Mollrich's bad breath and nondescript accent, as if these were pickup lines. Oliver's knee didn't agree with the rapid movement. It felt like his joint had been lined with sandpaper, grinding against itself, and a loud *snap* resonated through his body. He was used to a specific kind of knife-like pain—plunging from the outside in—but this time, he lost something, bursting from the inside out, as if his knee had finally ruptured.

Oliver leaned against the nearest wall and closed his eyes. The cute guy walked away without a goodbye. Oliver rolled up the cuff on his baggy gym shorts. A couple vines protruded from beneath his kneecap. On one vine, a pea-sized bud and two little white flowers emerged. He called over the physical therapist before completely collapsing and passing out.

Following some inconclusive tests, Oliver was prescribed a new painkiller cocktail. By nightfall, the bud had opened, and a few new vines snaked around the old ones. With each painful step during Oliver's day, the foliage grew a little denser, a new bud emerging every time the joint buckled. Most of the greenery came out clean, but some was slick with blood. He washed the vines and flowers in his bathtub and dabbed antibiotic ointment near the base of each protrusion.

At his next session, the physical therapist began by pinching two vines and moving them back and forth like miniature jump-ropes. "Keep manipulating the vines for two sets of twenty. We don't want the area to atrophy," he said. "I'll come back to check on you in a minute."

The cute guy showed up a few minutes later and began shoulder exercises in the opposite corner of the small gym. The cute guy glanced over at Oliver a couple times, but whenever Oliver looked back, the guy's eyes averted to the ceiling or floor. Oliver wasn't sure if he should be proud of his knee's new outgrowth or if he should hide it.

Oliver finished up the day with some lunges. When his knee cocked into its ninety-degree position, he felt something slip, and a thick vine shot directly out of the kneecap, hoisting a mass of cartilage, yanking out a glistening surgical pin with it. Oliver screamed, but despite the gruesome display, the pain wasn't much worse than usual. He hoped that the cute guy might come help him—or at least look up. He didn't.

The physical therapist removed the metal pin with some tweezers and deposited it in a plastic bag. He recommended ice, then heat, then Roundup weed killer.

That weekend, the cute guy wasn't there. Oliver ignored most of his physical therapist's commands, half-assing his way through the day's work. He refused to even bother with the pulley contraption. "Who is that guy with the AC problem?" Oliver asked.

"What do you mean who is he? He's a patient," the physical therapist said.

"Yeah, but what's his deal? Do you guys talk during his sessions? Does he live around here?"

"I don't know, man. Go ask him yourself next Monday."

"Oh, so he comes in every Monday?"

"Come on, just drop it. I can get fired for even letting that slip. HIPAA regulations. Just do your leg lifts and let's call it a day. Remember to ice it when you get home." Oliver did as he was told. Vines curled over the ice pack and drew it inward.

Oliver freed the ice pack with some gardening shears, then he took a hot shower. His knee throbbed, and the vines wiggled in time with his pulse. Back and forth, they jostled to the beat of his blood, almost like they were dancing.

On Monday, Oliver bought some better fitting gym shorts. He combed his hair—something he hadn't done in years. He placed a Listerine breath strip on his tongue, but he didn't like the taste, so he ate a spoonful of peanut butter to overpower the flavor.

The physical therapist set Oliver in motion, and the rest of the session took care of itself. He exercised in silence, flowing through his routine as if his knee were brand new and pain free. However, the blood dripping down his vine-riddled leg suggested otherwise. In time, blood streaked the floor, creating wide swatches of color in the otherwise monochromatic gym space. Oliver kept his eyes locked on the door, waiting for the now-tardy cute guy.

When the cute guy finally showed up, he exercised with some elastic bands for a while, manipulating his shoulder and wincing at each rotation. Oliver tried to rehearse what he might say, but nothing came to mind. He tried to remember some detail about Dr. Mollrich, but the man might've been a faceless gray blob for all Oliver knew. He couldn't focus. His nervous pulse caused the vines to shimmy and shake and spritz some pus onto the already lightly glazed floor. He mentally rehearsed: *Hi, my name's Oliver*, was the best he could imagine. He began mouthing the words. Then he voiced them for good measure. "I already know your name," the physical therapist said. Oliver hadn't realized anybody was in earshot. The physical therapist shook his head and went to his office for some insurance paperwork.

The cute guy dabbed his forehead with a towel, then he took off his windbreaker, revealing a beautiful cluster of greenery on his shoulder. "Holy shit!" Oliver muttered to himself. He hurried over to the cute guy, eager to take advantage of this newfound commonality.

A couple steps from the cute guy and Oliver's knee popped. Another pin shot out, and the destabilized limb went limp. Oliver slid across the floor and reached out, grasping anything that might brace his fall. He clung to the cute guy's T-shirt and they both toppled into a rack of yoga mats.

"Hi, my name's Oliver."

"What the fuck? Get off me," the cute guy said. He shoved Oliver, but nothing happened. Oliver could feel the force against his skin. He wasn't bracing himself or resisting, yet there was no give, no movement.

The cute guy pulled at the bundle of intertwined vines, writhing from separated shoulder to damaged knee. The mess of greenery wouldn't budge. A few white and red flowers blossomed, and lush stalks formed tight spirals. The vines melded into a series of mightier branches in a matter of seconds—it reminded Oliver of those flash-forward sequences on *Planet Earth*, David Attenborough prattling about the changing seasons. Leaves began unfurling. The two became one in a more literal sense than Oliver had envisioned.

"We're not liable for any injuries," the physical therapist said, emerging from his office. "Read the release forms."

"Can you call Dr. Mollrich, please?" The cute guy asked.

"So what's your name?" Oliver asked, completely ignoring the gap since his last awkward sentence.

The cute guy rubbed his temples. "I have a headache."

"I have Tylenol in my pocket," Oliver offered. The cute guy swallowed a couple pills and finally answered, "Ryan."

"Nice to meet you."

"Yeah, whatever."

"How long have your vines been growing?" Oliver asked.

"A couple days."

"I've had mine for a week or so."

"Shit, so it doesn't go away?" Ryan asked.

Oliver shook his head.

Dr. Mollrich pulled at the vines and huffed his rancid breath into Oliver's face. He poked the flowers with a tongue depressor. He listened to a pod with his stethoscope. After a few minutes of examination, Dr. Mollrich decided to call an expert from some hospital in Denver. "He knows all about Siamese twins."

"I think they're called conjoined twins," Oliver said.

"We're not twins," Ryan said.

"Nevertheless, you're fused together, so I think Dr. Abbott can help."

The physical therapist brought Oliver and Ryan a bag of McDonald's for dinner. Oliver tried to remain solemn—after all, this was a medical emergency—but he couldn't stave off the occasional smile. The bag of greasy fast food was tantamount to a first date, and he was determined to make the most of it.

"Where did you grow up?" Oliver asked.

"Close by. Near Pueblo," Ryan said.

After a while of waiting for Ryan to lob the question back, Oliver volunteered his own answer: "I grew up in Portland. It's nice there. Lots of trees."

"Sure, okay," Ryan said, fishing through the bag for more ketchup.

"What do you do for work?"

"I manage a hotel. You?"

Oliver couldn't picture this standoffish guy in the hospitality trade, but he was glad that the conversation was turning into a real back-and-forth. "I work in marketing," Oliver said. "But not regular marketing. Guerrilla marketing. Grassroots stuff."

Ryan nodded and slurped some Diet Coke.

"Family?" Oliver asked.

Ryan didn't answer.

"What TV shows do you like?" Oliver asked.

"Just because we're stuck together doesn't mean we need to chitchat."

"Okay, I just thought maybe we could watch something. You know, to pass the time," Oliver said. "I have an iPad in my gym bag. I bet the physical therapist can grab it for us."

Ryan finally smiled. They watched back-to-back episodes of *Better Call Saul*. Oliver shifted as much of his body as possible amid the vine outgrowth, resting his head on Ryan's right shoulder. Oliver expected to be shooed away, but Ryan didn't mind—or maybe he didn't notice. In either case, Oliver nuzzled closer. He watched the vines twisting over their bodies while Ryan watched the glowing screen.

Dr. Abbott interrupted just as Oliver felt he might be able to ask a couple more questions, or maybe even sneak a kiss. Dr. Abbott's nimble fingers wiggled between the vines. He plucked a few representative petals and leaves. He rubbed his chin and mumbled "I see…" a couple times.

"And you say there's no history of vine outgrowth in your family?"

Oliver and Ryan both shook their heads.

"And no history of Siamese twins?" Dr. Abbott asked. Dr. Mollrich crossed his arms, likely pleased that this expert was using his same out-of-date and politically incorrect terminology.

"No. And we're not twins."

"I see," Dr. Abbott said. He rubbed his chin some more. "I think I know somebody who can help."

"Dr. Singh?" Dr. Mollrich asked.

"No."

"Hayes? Pak?"

"No, not a doctor. His name's Craig. He did landscaping for me last summer. Good guy. Great rates. Quality work. He can get these vines cleared right up. I'll give him a ring, but I doubt he can come right away. I'll see about tomorrow morning."

"How the hell do we get home?" Ryan asked.

"You don't," the physical therapist said. He flicked one particularly thick vine with his index finger. The vine had woven itself into the floor, breaking through tile and concrete. Smaller offshoots clung to exposed pipes and wrapped around nearby workout gear, and one spindly branch snuck skyward, curling around a light fixture.

"Great, so I'm stuck with this guy all night?" Ryan asked.

Oliver brushed off the callous comment and nuzzled a bit closer. Ryan wiggled a bit, perhaps trying to inch away despite the vines holding them together. Oliver suggested they watch more TV, but Ryan wanted to get to bed. Oliver considered what he might say tomorrow, once they were separated. *Want to grab a coffee sometime? How about we watch more Better Call Saul this weekend?* If all else failed, maybe he'd feign professional interest, suggesting that he look over the marketing plan at Ryan's hotel.

They ate McDonald's breakfast sandwiches in silence. Ryan slurped his black coffee, while Oliver drank his two-cream, two-sugar blend in slower, deliberate gulps. Craig was punctual, arriving shortly after the physical therapist had delivered the food.

"Alright, let's see what we've got," Craig said, opening a yellow toolbox.

"Will this hurt?" Oliver asked.

"Nah, no more than physical therapy," Craig said. He patted his left shoulder. "I messed up my shoulder a few years

Physical Therapy

ago. Rough stuff. I feel for you guys."

"Oh yeah?" Ryan said. "I hurt my shoulder too. AC joint separation. You?"

"Torn rotator cuff," Craig said. He retrieved a gigantic, hooked saw and began slicing through the thickest outgrowths.

"Man, too bad," Ryan said. The two began chatting. They both took their coffee black, and they both watched *Better Call Saul* and *Mayans*, and they both hated McDonald's, and Oliver hated every minute of their chummy banter.

The vines and roots and branches and leaves fell away in a series of buzz-cuts and snips and snaps and slices. Blood and sap bubbled from various trimmings, each becoming shriveled and useless within minutes of being excised. The procedure didn't seem to cause Ryan any pain, but Oliver felt each cut. It wasn't as bad as physical therapy—that was true—but it wasn't painless. Each time a vine died, a cold prickly sensation washed over Oliver's body. By the time it was over, he was numb, barely able to move, as if his whole body had atrophied in the time they had spent conjoined and motionless. He remained curled and lifeless as Ryan stood and cleaned off layers of sawdust and clipped leaves. Ryan inspected his once vine-ridden shoulder and found nothing but fresh, pink skin.

"Give me a call sometime," Ryan said. He gave Craig a business card.

Craig said, "Yeah, sure" and pocketed the card.

They both left, but Oliver remained on the floor until the lights went out. "Time to go," the physical therapist said.

Oliver moved his stiff limbs. His knee felt a little better. Maybe the range of motion was improving after all. He brushed sawdust and pulpy residue off his clothes. He picked through the decaying vines still strewn across the floor, searching for any piece that might still be green and alive.

Karol's Cleaners Will Clean Anything

That's what the sign says. When asked, Karol confirms, "Yes, anything. Read the sign, dipshit."

I normally wash my veggies at home, but these greens need professional help. The kale is dirty and limp, the broccoli is buggy. I load the nearest machine and add off-brand detergent. I set the gigantic dial to *fruits/vegetables* and deposit quarters. After a thirty-minute cycle, the greens are clean, plump, and crispy.

Back home, I chop my cleaned veggies. I realize I'm surrounded by other dirty things. A blackened skillet, a permanently stained Tupperware container, a blender with gunk stuck in every crevasse. I return to Karol's. I set the dial: *miscellaneous hard objects*. After forty-five minutes, each item shines anew.

I smile and laugh. "This is amazing," I exclaim to the woman next to me. She scowls and moves her body in front of her washer, trying to block my view. She's cleaning a stack of envelopes emblazoned with words like *Final Notice* and *Past Due*.

Karol lowers her newspaper and says, "Don't bother the other customers, dipshit. People could be washing their unmentionables."

"Sorry, I didn't realize."

"That's no excuse," Karol says. She mumbles something else—probably calls me a dipshit again.

I take my polished kitchenware home, and I scramble to find other washables. I pull down dusty curtains. I roll up my white rug with its deep wine stains. I grab muddied camping gear.

Toward the back of my coat closet, I stumble upon the box you gave me. I used to look inside regularly, but now I've almost forgotten what it contains. Mom's wedding ring. The poem she wrote Dad for their thirtieth. Her hospital bracelet. Lots of photographs, mostly of us kids. Mom was often behind the camera rather than in front of it—a family historian unable to catalogue herself. The photos are yellowing. They need cleaning.

I go back to Karol's Cleaners. Karol lowers her paper again, but she doesn't call me a dipshit. She sees the box in my trembling hands. "Remember, we clean anything," she says. Her voice is gentle.

I set the dial to my name and climb into the washing machine. The drum aches under my weight, but it begins to spin. Water gushes. Thick foam rises.

Tuxedos and Evening Gowns

When I open my bedroom door, there's always someone inside, dressed to the nines. I've tested this phenomenon a couple dozen times so far. I don't know where these bedroom people come from. My room doesn't have windows. There's only one way in or out. I can shut the door on the windowless room, wait a few minutes, open the door, and *voilà*. They nod appreciatively and walk out. I get the impression that they're waiting for me, waiting to be let out. But it's not like some panicky incarceration. These people are always calm and collected. Their tuxedos and evening gowns are pristine. Their hair and makeup is flawless. They're waiting, but not quite trapped.

They rarely say anything to me, these people in my room. Sometimes they offer a polite "good evening" or "nice weather we're having." Whenever I try to talk directly to them, they smile and look somewhat uncomfortable, as if their politeness can only extend to the most rudimentary phraseology. I say, "Pardon me, could you please tell me why you're in my room?" I'm not sure why I bother with these niceties—there's something about their fancy clothes that encourages civility, I guess. After about one week of good manners, I drop the decorum and insist: "Tell me right now! How did you get in here?"

These people shudder at my lack of grace, and their voices quaver as they say "good day" in a hurry. They brush past me, their expensive-smelling colognes and perfumes lingering in the air. They appear more agitated now, but they never break from their politeness. They always close the door behind them, and I'm left in my dimly-lit hovel with my stained mattress, 90s band posters on the wall, IKEA side table, alarm clock on the blink.

I try to follow them out, but they catch a never-ending series of buses and trains, and I always lose them after the fifth or sixth transfer. I sleuth for a couple weeks. Every time, they vanish into midday commuter crowds only to reappear on some distant bus as it chugs forward, leaving me on the platform by myself.

I decide that they're embarrassed by my hoodie and jeans. If I look like I belong, maybe I'll be able to make all the correct transfers. Maybe I can attend whatever swanky party is waiting at the end-o'-the-line. So I dress myself to the nines—tuxedo, shiny leather shoes, bowtie. I trim my beard. I gel my hair. I look *gooooood*. I stand in the middle of the room—I want to sit on my stained mattress, but I can't risk messing up my new clothes. I watch the door, and I know somebody will let me out soon. I will nod at this person and say "good day" in my most polite voice. I will leave the room, and I will know exactly where I am going.

Acknowledgments

Thank you to the editors of the following journals and magazines who originally published early versions of these stories:

A cappella Zoo: "Physical Therapy";
Black Lily: "My Fingernails Are Haunted";
F(r)iction: "Tuxedos and Evening Gowns";
Ghost Parachute: "Karol's Cleaners Will Clean Anything";
Juked: "The Museum of Future Mistakes";
Literary Orphans: "Kitten Egg";
Maudlin House: "The Last Dinosaurs of Portland";
Monkeybicycle: "Sharon's Lover is Dissipating";
Okay Donkey: "When the Astronauts Landed in Our Neighborhood";
Paper Darts: "Kitchenly Perfection" (published as "The Renovation");
Please Hold Magazine: "Evolution of Apartments";
SmokeLong Quarterly: "The Gull Bone Index" (published as "Determining the Gull Bone Index");
The Collapsar: "Hospital Story";
The Coil: "Sharon's Lover is Dissipating" (reprint);
Variant Literature: "Brother and Not-Brother."

The story "Karol's Cleaners Will Clean Anything" was anthologized in *Best Microfiction 2023*, published by Pelekinesis in 2023. The stories "Migratory Patterns" and "The Last Dinosaurs of Portland" appeared in the chapbook, *The Last Dinosaurs of Portland*, published by Bottlecap Press in 2021. "Fruit Rot" appeared as a standalone novelette, *Fruit Rot*, published by Etchings Press at the University of Indianapolis in 2020.

Thank you to everyone at BOA Editions who helped transform *The Museum of Future Mistakes* from a manuscript into a finished book: Justine Alfano, Amy Betti, Peter Conners, Sandy Knight, and Isabella Madeira. Thank you to Tim Z. Hernandez, Margaret Malone, and Ren Powell for offering guidance and feedback on early drafts from this collection. And of course, thanks to my loving wife Uma Sankaram for being there for me during the stressful, exciting, and beautiful process of writing and publishing this thing.

About the Author

James R. Gapinski (they/them) is the author of the novella *Edge of the Known Bus Line*—winner of the 2018 Etchings Press Novella Prize, named to *Kirkus Reviews*' Best Books of 2018, and a finalist for the 2019 Montaigne Medal. James is also the author of three fiction chapbooks, and their short work has appeared in the *Best Microfiction 2023* anthology, *HAD*, *Heavy Feather Review*, *SmokeLong Quarterly*, *Variant Literature*, and other publications. *The Museum of Future Mistakes* is their first full-length collection. They live in Portland, Oregon with their wife and cats.

BOA Editions, Ltd.
American Reader Series

No. 1   *Christmas at the Four Corners of the Earth*
Prose by Blaise Cendrars
Translated by Bertrand Mathieu

No. 2   *Pig Notes & Dumb Music: Prose on Poetry*
By William Heyen

No. 3   *After-Images: Autobiographical Sketches*
By W. D. Snodgrass

No. 4   *Walking Light: Memoirs and Essays on Poetry*
By Stephen Dunn

No. 5   *To Sound Like Yourself: Essays on Poetry*
By W. D. Snodgrass

No. 6   *You Alone Are Real to Me: Remembering Rainer Maria Rilke*
By Lou Andreas-Salomé

No. 7   *Breaking the Alabaster Jar: Conversations with Li-Young Lee*
Edited by Earl G. Ingersoll

No. 8   *I Carry A Hammer In My Pocket For Occasions Such As These*
By Anthony Tognazzini

No. 9   *Unlucky Lucky Days*
By Daniel Grandbois

No. 10   *Glass Grapes and Other Stories*
By Martha Ronk

No. 11   *Meat Eaters & Plant Eaters*
By Jessica Treat

No. 12   *On the Winding Stair*
By Joanna Howard

No. 13   *Cradle Book*
By Craig Morgan Teicher

No. 14   *In the Time of the Girls*
By Anne Germanacos

No. 15   *This New and Poisonous Air*
By Adam McOmber

No. 16   *To Assume a Pleasing Shape*
By Joseph Salvatore

No. 17   *The Innocent Party*
By Aimee Parkison

No. 18   *Passwords Primeval: 20 American Poets in Their Own Words*
Interviews by Tony Leuzzi

No. 19   *The Era of Not Quite*
By Douglas Watson

No. 20   *The Winged Seed: A Remembrance*
By Li-Young Lee

No. 21   *Jewelry Box: A Collection of Histories*
By Aurelie Sheehan

No. 22   *The Tao of Humiliation*
By Lee Upton

No. 23   *Bridge*
By Robert Thomas

No. 24   *Reptile House*
By Robin McLean

No. 25   *The Education of a Poker Player*
James McManus

No. 26   *Remarkable*
By Dinah Cox

No. 27   *Gravity Changes*
By Zach Powers

No. 28   *My House Gathers Desires*
By Adam McOmber

No. 29   *An Orchard in the Street*
By Reginald Gibbons

No. 30   *The Science of Lost Futures*
By Ryan Habermeyer

No. 31   *Permanent Exhibit*
By Matthew Vollmer

No. 32   *The Rapture Index: A Suburban Bestiary*
By Molly Reid

No. 33   *Joytime Killbox*
By Brian Wood

No. 34   *The OK End of Funny Town*
By Mark Polanzak

No. 35   *The Complete Writings of Art Smith, The Bird Boy of Fort Wayne, Edited by Michael Martone*
By Michael Martone

No. 36 *Alien Stories*
By E.C. Osondu
No. 37 *Among Elms, in Ambush*
By Bruce Weigl
No. 38 *Are We Ever Our Own*
By Gabrielle Lucille Fuentes
No. 39 *The Visibility of Things Long Submerged*
By George Looney
No. 40 *Where Can I Take You When There's Nowhere To Go*
By Joe Baumann
No. 41 *Exile in Guyville*
By Amy Lee Lillard
No. 42 *Black Buffalo Woman*
By Kazim Ali
No. 43 *Radical Red*
By Nathan Dixon
No. 44 *The Museum of Future Mistakes*
By James R. Gapinski

Colophon

BOA Editions, Ltd., a nonprofit publisher of poetry and other literary works, fosters readership and appreciation of contemporary literature. By identifying, cultivating, and publishing both new and established poets and selecting authors of unique literary talent, BOA brings high-quality literature to the public. Support for this effort comes from the sale of its publications, grant funding, and private donations.

———

The publication of this book is made possible, in part, by the special support of the following individuals:

Anonymous (x3)
Ralph Black & Susan Murphy
Angela Bonazinga & Catherine Lewis
Gwen Conners, *in memory of June Baker*
Chris Dahl, *in honor of Chuck Hertrick*
Bonnie Garner
James Hale
Grant Holcomb
Nora A. Jones
Joe & Dale Klein
Barbara Lovenheim, *in memory of John Lovenheim*
Joe McElveney
John & Judy Messenger
Daniel M. Meyers, *in honor of J. Shepard Skiff*
Dorrie Parini
Boo Poulin, *in memory of A. Poulin Jr.*
Michael Quattrone
Jim Robie & Edith Matthai, *in memory of Pexer Hursh*
Deborah Ronnen
John H. Schultz
William Waddell & Linda Rubel